LYDIA'S PASSION

•

Tracey J. Lyons

Text copyright ©2004 by Tracey J. Lyons
All rights reserved.
Printed in the United States of America.

Published by Montlake Romance
P.O. Box 400818
Las Vegas, NV 89140

ISBN-13: 9781477811641
ISBN-10: 1477811648

For the Wild Women:
Linda, Patty, Lori, and Penny.
Thanks for keeping me laughing!

Chapter One

Catskill Mountains
Surprise, New York
1882

The entire calamity could have been so much worse. Of course, certain people were making more out of the mishap than was necessary. Thankfully, no injuries were sustained, unless one counted a little wounded pride.

"Have you gone blind, woman?"

Lydia stared, seeing clearly the red-faced man shouting and waving his arms about wildly in front of her.

"I beg your pardon, sir, but I can see just fine!" Lydia dropped down from the buggy seat. Gently,

1

she patted the horse's long neck, quickly quieting the brown mare hitched to the buggy.

Pulling his hat low on his brow, he narrowed his eyes to look down his nose at her. "I should have known it would be one of you!" Placing his hands on his narrow hips, he continued to stare at her.

"What's that supposed to mean?"

"You're one of Miss Margaret's nieces."

His response, which came out sounding more like a snarl than civil words, insulted Lydia.

Lifting her chin up a notch and mustering up her meanest stare, she looked right at him. "I do have a name. It's Lydia Monroe. Do you have a problem with my being one of her relatives?"

He seemed to back off just a bit. Still not acting quite as contrite as she would have liked, he said, "The only problem I have is with people like you coming through this town at breakneck speed."

Pretending to ponder his comment, she patiently folded her hands. Sunlight bounced off the high polish of the black buggy. It was a fine day to be out for a ride. Tired of being cooped up after days of nothing but gray cloudy skies, Lydia had jumped at the chance to run to town for a few notions.

She could have walked the short distance, but making a grand entrance with her Aunt Margaret's new buggy seemed so much more exciting. Not to mention that the deep blue color of her new day gown looked strikingly elegant against the tufted black leather seat.

The blue bonnet that had arrived in last week's post sat atop her perfectly combed hair. Lydia had even gone to the trouble of putting on her leather riding gloves. One never knew who one would run into in Surprise these days. What with the onslaught of newcomers, a young woman of marrying age could never be too prepared to bump into the next handsome bachelor to come to town.

Of course she wasn't really in the market for a husband. Lydia liked being a free spirit. Knowing there was still plenty of time left in her life to find the perfect mate brought a smile to her lips. It delighted her to no end knowing that her fine mane of red hair brought more than one appreciative stare from the brawnier sex.

Her flirtations were harmless fun.

It was while she'd been having those thoughts that a brown rabbit had bounded out of the tall grass lining the roadway causing Lydia to jerk the reins of the horse hard to the right in an effort to avoid hitting the adorable creature. The horse must have been going a bit faster than she'd thought, for the next thing she knew, the buggy had gone careening around the corner in front of the new school building.

In an effort to explain all of this, she said

calmly, "I'll have you know, Mr. Judson—" oh yes indeed—she knew who this young man was with the wavy brown hair and deep dark brown eyes. "A poor innocent creature was saved because of my quick reflexes."

His face reddened and he began to sputter. "I'll have you know, Miss Lydia Monroe, that your reflexes almost killed me!"

Rolling her eyes heavenward, she sighed. "Really there's no need to exaggerate what happened."

The nerve of the man! It was just a silly little near—accident. It wasn't her fault he'd been standing in the middle of the road looking in the opposite direction.

Gently, she chided, "Perhaps *you* were the one in the way."

Alexander Judson had just finished pounding the last nail into a piece of door trim on the schoolhouse. He and his partner Cole Stanton had been working six days a week for the past month putting the finishing details on the project. The Judson Lumber Company was his business. A month ago, he'd taken Cole on as his partner. It seemed a good fit considering the man could work magic with a simple piece of wood. True craftsmanship like his didn't come along everyday.

The job was completed one week shy of the start of the school year. He was the head of Surprise's school committee and had as yet to find a teacher. He supposed things would come together all in good time. With the demands on his growing business, new orders coming in as fast as he got them out the door, and taking care of his two children and the housework, it was no wonder he'd been unable to find a teacher. There just weren't enough hours in his day.

Taking a step back from the front door, he stood on the edge of what would soon be the play yard and admired the handiwork. It was a sturdy building, one that housed not one, but two good-sized classrooms. They'd built desks, enough so each student could have their own, and Cole had surprised him with an additional five this morning, just in case.

The chairs had been donated by Margaret Monroe Sinclair, self-appointed matriarch of the town of Surprise. As much as Alexander thought she was a meddlesome busybody, he had to admit that Miss Margaret was generous to a fault when it came to her town.

Those were the thoughts running through his head when this woman with her brilliant red hair and flashy blue dress nearly took his life!

And now said woman had the audacity to stand before him denying her part in the incident. As far as he was concerned, she had no business handling anything with wheels attached to it, let alone a brand new buggy.

"I think it might be a good idea if you walked, rather than drove, your horse the rest of the way into Surprise."

It seemed a logical suggestion to him, but he could tell by the look on her face and the spark in those green eyes that shimmered like emeralds, that she was going to argue his point.

Carefully, she folded her arms, eyeing him with intent. Alexander held his breath, preparing for what he suspected would be a long steady stream of angry words.

"You know something, Mr. Judson? You are an insolent man, one who I've already wasted enough of my precious time on. Good day!"

As simple as that, with a quick turn and a flounce of blue skirts, she jumped into the buggy and rode off to town. Rubbing a hand over his jaw, he was tempted to shout "Good riddance!" to her retreating back. Shaking his head, he decided it best to keep his mouth shut.

He'd already wasted enough time having this little exchange with Miss Margaret's niece. The first of the three nieces had arrived in town earlier this year. Abigail Monroe Stanton was the sheriff and married to his partner. Lydia came soon after, and Maggie arrived last.

Walking back to the schoolhouse entrance, he

started gathering his tools. Abigail and Cole had gotten off to quite the rocky start. First, she'd arrested him for drunk and disorderly behavior, and then she'd kept him in jail on a mistaken burglary charge. It had all come out in the wash in the end, though. Eventually Cole's innocence was proven and the two fell head over heels in love.

Putting the hammer and bag of nails in the wooden toolbox, Alex shook his head in wonder. Through it all Cole had kept his cool, even helping to apprehend the real criminal, who turned out to be a poor misguided woman named Wanda McGurdy. Alex heard she was spending the next five years in a women's prison in Albany.

"Hey, what did Lydia want?" Cole stepped out of the cool interior of the building.

Setting the toolbox on the step, Alex looked up at him and grumbled, "She wanted to run me over."

Cole grinned. "I take it this means she had the new buggy out for a ride."

"You could say that. She darn near killed me! She said she was trying to avoid hitting some innocent creature."

"Innocent creature?"

"Her words not mine." Standing, Alex picked up the toolbox. Pride swelled as he looked at what the Judson Lumber Company had accomplished. "I'd say this school is ready for the children."

Glancing around, Cole agreed. "All it needs is a teacher. Any luck in finding one yet?"

Together the men walked down the pathway to the road. "I haven't had a chance to interview anyone yet. Miss Margaret keeps telling me that she has the perfect candidate. Honestly, with this building and my two children, I haven't had time to meet this person."

Cole gave him a knowing smile. "I'd be careful if I were you. Miss Margaret always finds a way to get what she wants."

Alex knew Cole was speaking from experience. The woman had been instrumental in bringing all three of her nieces here and in helping Cole and Abigail find their way to each other. Even though Miss Margaret kept mostly to herself in the big house at the end of town, she still managed to know just about everything that was going on in Surprise.

"If you want to head home, I can close up the office." Cole's offer came at the end of another long day and normally Alexander would have gone back to the lumberyard and closed up himself. Today, though, he was grateful for the offer.

"I'd like to get home at a reasonable hour. It's been a long time since I've read a bedtime story to my kids. Thanks. I'll see you in the morning. Tell the sheriff I said hello."

"Will do."

Following the pathway that wound its way between the schoolhouse and his lumberyard, Alex walked home feeling as if he'd accomplished a great deal. And yet there was still a hollow place inside of him.

His wife, Joanna, had died in a tragic accident two years ago. It happened right at the edge of their property. What began as an innocent family picnic ended with his wife's death.

They'd made plans to meet under the big oak tree near the pond. He'd been catching up on lumber orders and was late. Joanna had climbed the tree to free their son Robert's kite. The branch snapped under her weight. He found her lying on the ground, her life already gone.

Most men would have quickly found a mate if for nothing more than to raise the children. Knowing he couldn't bear the heartbreak of another loss like that, he'd taken what he thought was the easy way out—choosing to bury himself in his work.

As a result, he was working fourteen hour days and returning home most nights in a surly mood to find his son and daughter tucked in bed. He promised himself tonight would be different. He would celebrate the completion of the schoolhouse by taking his evening meal with Laura and Robert, then reading them their favorite bedtime stories.

The sound of their laughter reached him before the two-story house came into view. He smiled in spite of himself. It was a comforting sound, a sound that signified home. He spotted them first. The two were playing a game of tag. When he came up over the rise in front of his yard, he saw that Robert was about to tag his younger sister.

Their laughter stopped when they saw him. Robert and Laura stood side by side, looking up at him expectantly, their smiles all but gone from their little faces.

"There's no need to stop your game." He spoke softly, as if seeing them for the first time. Robert was growing so fast that the hem of the pants Alexander bought him just two months ago was already creeping up his leg. And Laura needed new shoes. He could see where her toes were wearing the leather thin.

"Papa, you're home so soon?" Robert slowly made his way to his father with Laura walking along beside him.

The way they were reacting to his early arrival gave Alexander pause. Was he such a bad father that his children feared him? He hoped not. The only thing they had left in this world was each other. Looking at his children, he reminded himself that he worked long hours to provide a decent home for them.

During the time he was gone, the grandmotherly widow Mrs. Sutherland cared for them. She'd recently taken up residence in one of the new homes built on Elm Street. Hearing him approach, she stepped out onto the porch.

"Good to see you home early, Mr. Judson."

Turning towards her, he couldn't keep the pride from his voice. "We finished the school today."

"That's wonderful news! Did you hear what your papa said? Your school is done!"

Laura clambered up into his arms. "Is that true, Papa?"

Her tiny hands framed his face. Looking into Laura's blue eyes reminded him of her mother, Joanna. The ache in his heart had slowly diminished over the past two years until it was nearly gone.

"Yes. Mr. Stanton and I pounded the last nail in today."

Giving Laura a quick hug, he set her back on the ground.

"I hear there's even a new teacher," Mrs. Sutherland said while smoothing down the front of Laura's dress.

"I don't know about that. The school committee hasn't completed the interviews." Alexander put his arm around his son's shoulders. "How are you doing, son?"

Big brown eyes looked up at him. "Good, Pa'. Does this mean we have to go to school?"

Alex smiled. It seemed his son wasn't too keen

on the idea of some schooling. "Yes, you and Laura are both going to the new school." Seeing the doubt in Robert's eyes, he added, "All of your friends will be there. You can see them everyday. Trust me, it'll be fun."

"What if we get a mean teacher?"

"Don't forget I'm doing the hiring. So I promise no mean teacher."

"Mr. Judson, your teacher may have already been chosen." Mrs. Sutherland persisted.

Turning from his son, he looked at her. "I don't think so. How can that be when I haven't even interviewed anyone for the job?"

"Oh, I think you know the answer to that question, Mr. Judson."

Groaning he went into the house.

"I think the contents of this envelope will explain everything." She handed him the expensive cream colored envelope.

Turning it over right away he noticed the seal. The wax seal had been stamped with the letter "S". This could only mean one thing—Miss Margaret was involved. With trepidation, he opened the envelope, and taking out the single sheet of stationery, quickly read the neatly scripted words.

Mr. Judson,
*   You will find your new teacher at the school-house tomorrow morning at 9:00 o'clock. I'm*

quite certain you will find this young woman meets all of your requirements. I'm glad I could be of service.
Sincerely,
Margaret Monroe Sinclair

Chapter Two

Lydia didn't know what to think. Alexander Judson was a handsome man by her standards. She couldn't figure out why he'd been so rude to her. It's not like she'd actually injured him in any way. The buggy hadn't touched him—though thinking about it now, she thought it was possible that it might have lightly grazed him.

Still, in the end there was no harm done. And hadn't she looked attractive in her blue dress and new bonnet? At the very least the man could have tipped his hat to her when she'd taken her leave. Lydia wasn't used to being ignored by men and Mr. Judson's actions had left her ego feeling a tad bruised.

But why should this bother her, she wondered?

There were plenty of men in Surprise whose heads turned when she passed by. Alexander Judson just didn't happen to be one of them. Fine by her. From here on out, she'd pay no attention to him!

Handing the reins off to Aunt Margaret's stable boy, Lydia went inside the house.

"Oh, there you are! Miss Margaret was wondering where you went off to," Anna said, giving her the usual pinch-faced smile.

"I took the buggy out for a ride." Handing her bonnet to the tall, thin housekeeper, Lydia decided to find her aunt.

"Miss Margaret is in the sitting room," Anna told her.

It was uncanny the way Anna knew what people were thinking. "Thank you, Anna. Is there tea?" Lydia thought a good cup of tea might improve her mood.

"I just took a fresh pot to Miss Margaret."

Just entering the sitting room and seeing her aunt in one of the wing-backed chairs in front of the fireplace, rather than in her wheelchair, made Lydia feel better. Aunt Margaret had been ill with an undiagnosed malady for quite some time; it was the reason Lydia had come to stay with her.

"Lydia. Come, sit, have a cup of this lovely tea that Anna made. I've some news for you."

After pouring two cups of tea, Lydia sat in the

opposite chair, anxious to hear what her aunt had to say.

"As you know the school committee has been seeking an appropriate candidate to fill the position of schoolteacher."

Swallowing her mouthful of tea, Lydia nodded, wondering what this had to do with her.

"I believe the school is finished, and we'd like to have the children behind those desks as soon as possible. It's imperative that we find the right person."

"That makes sense to me, Aunt Margaret. A proper education is important." Lydia agreed. "And yes, the children should be in school as soon as possible."

Clapping her hands together, Aunt Margaret said, "Oh, I'm so relieved to hear you say that because, my dear Lydia, you will be the person guiding these young minds into the future!"

Sputtering, and then choking on her tea, Lydia could hardly find the words to speak. "You can't be serious!"

"You'll do fine. The head of the committee will meet you at the school tomorrow morning at nine o'clock."

Placing the tea cup and saucer on the table between them, Lydia quickly stood up. "You can't be serious. I don't know a thing about teaching! I'm sorry Aunt, but I can't do it."

Raising her hands to her forehead, Aunt Margaret began to massage her temples. "I hate it when these headaches come on. This one just seemed to hit from right out of nowhere."

Immediately Lydia felt horribly guilty at the possibility of being the cause of the spell. Springing from her seat at the sight of her aunt's pale face, she panicked. "Let me go get Anna!"

Rushing out into the hallway Lydia shouted, "Anna! Anna, come quickly!"

The housekeeper came running from the back of the house, her face flushed from the sudden exertion. "What is it?"

"Aunt Margaret is having one of those headaches." Lydia followed along as Anna swept ahead of her into the sitting room.

Going to Aunt Margaret's side, Anna put her hand to the older woman's forehead. "Miss Margaret, do you need me to fetch the doctor?"

Waving her hand in front of her face, it looked as if the pain might have subsided. "There's no need for hysterics. I'm much better now." Seeing the doubtful look on Lydia's face, she added, "Really I am. Come and sit back down, Lydia, so we can finish our conversation."

Going to her aunt's side, Lydia frowned down at her with concern. Giving in to Aunt Margaret's suggestion was not as hard as she'd thought. "If it's what you wish, I'll go to the school in the morning."

Taking her hand, Aunt Margaret gave Lydia a watery smile. "That would be wonderful, but only if it's what you want to do, my dear."

"It is." And with those two words, Lydia suddenly felt as if the rest of her life had been decided. She wanted to say it was unfair, but deep down she knew it was high time that she found a way to spend her days. Her cousins were busy most of the day and Lydia did find herself at loose ends more often than not.

Abigail had her hands full as a new wife and serving as the town's sheriff, and Maggie was working on ideas for a new dance hall. This left Lydia with plenty of idle time to fill.

Admittedly, teaching would not have been her first choice. Smiling in satisfaction, she asked herself, honestly, what harm could there be in giving lessons and shaping the minds of the town's youngsters?

Alexander was up before the sun. He enjoyed this quiet time to think about the day ahead. The children were still sleeping soundly and the town below the bluff was in a peaceful morning slumber. From where he sat on the front porch, he could see the roof of the schoolhouse. It should have been satisfying to know that the building was finished, that hours of hard work had finally paid off, but all Alex felt was anxious.

There was still the matter of finding the right person to teach the children. According to Mrs. Sutherland, Miss Margaret had someone in mind, someone who would meet him at the school in just a few short hours.

Tipping the white mug to his mouth, Alex drank the last dregs of his morning coffee. The sky was turning pink and ruby-toned as the sun began to rise over Surprise. Soon the town would come alive—Robert and Laura would be awake, wanting breakfast, and Walter Smith would be expecting the lumber order he placed for his new house last week to be cut and ready for delivery.

Mr. Jules had also requested some new shelving for the Mercantile. While Cole had made progress on the Smith order, Alex had yet to measure the space for the shelves. The school had taken priority. Today, though, that would all change. As soon as the teacher was hired, Alex would be able to return his attentions to his other clients.

Exactly three hours later, with the children fed and in the care of Mrs. Sutherland, he was out of the house on his way to the school. As he rounded the bend, the familiar white clapboard building came into view—and parked outside was a very familiar looking buggy. Miss Margaret apparently had come herself to introduce him to this remarkable person who wanted to teach at the school.

Wiping his feet on the mat carefully placed in front of the door, he entered the cool interior. The air still smelled of fresh cut lumber and wet paint. The wide floor planks had been swept clean and shafts of sunlight filtered through the tall windows lining the outside walls.

What caught his attention, though, was the woman standing in front of the chalkboard. As her back was to him, he admired her pleasing shape. Allowing his eyes to take in the sight, his breath caught somewhere between an inhale and an exhale. How could he have missed all of that red hair? His high hopes for having a decent day plummeted like a rock sinking in a deep lake.

Hearing his footsteps, she turned around. He caught the brilliant smile just before it faded from her face.

"You! What are you doing here?" Lydia Monroe pulled herself up to her full height, which by Alexander's quick estimation couldn't have been much more than five feet.

Taking his hat off, Alexander eyed her coolly. "I might ask the same question of you, Miss Monroe." He walked to the front of the classroom, stopping when he reached the end of the aisle.

Taking a bold step toward him, she said, "I'm here to meet with the head of the school committee."

Raising her perfectly arched eyebrows, she added, "My aunt sent me down here to see about the teaching position."

This couldn't be happening. Alexander felt as if his world were spinning out of control. The children of this town needed someone with a firm hand, a woman who was of spinster age, settled in life, and looking for no more than to impart her hard-earned knowledge to young minds.

Lydia Monroe was *not* that woman.

Why, she was the total opposite of what he was looking for. Bold, defiant, and the color of her hair was all wrong. A red-headed teacher wasn't at all what he'd envisioned. And she was young, much too young. He'd bet she wasn't even twenty years old.

Shaking his head, he said, "No. No. No!" Extending his arm, he pointed back towards the door. "You go back home and tell your aunt that I'm not having any of her interfering in this decision."

"How dare you? You're not only insulting me, but you're insulting my aunt by throwing her good deeds back in her face. She's a sick woman, Mr. Judson, and I will not be the one to tell her how ungrateful you are. You can go do that yourself." Fury in flight, she stomped by him. Stopping a few inches past him, she spun around and looked at him. "What gives you the right to turn down my aunt's offer?"

"I'm the head of the school committee."

What he was sure would have been a scathing retort was cut off as a tall figure filled the doorway.

"Mr. Judson, I'm glad to catch you here."

Walter Smith stepped from the shadows, his lumberjack bulk practically filling the space between the two desks where he stood.

"Mr. Smith, if you've come to see me about your lumber order, I believe that Cole is going to be handling it," Alex said.

"No, no. I came in when I saw the buggy parked out front, hoping to meet our new teacher." Advancing into the room, he doffed his hat and smiled at Miss Monroe. "Nice to meet you, ma'am."

"It's nice to meet you, too, Mr. Smith." Lydia beamed up at the man, not bothering to mention the fact that she hadn't been hired.

Alexander fumed at the deceit and was about to correct the misassumption when Mrs. Leland White entered the building. She and her husband had four rambunctious youngsters and had been pestering Alex for more than two weeks hoping he'd hired someone for the job. Alex imagined she needed the quiet that the school hours would bring her.

Clapping her hands together, she pounced. "Did I hear correctly, Mr. Smith, this is our new teacher?"

"Yes, Mrs. White. This young lady is the new teacher. Mr. Judson I'm glad to see you finally found the time to hire her."

He was fast losing control of the situation. These people mistakenly assumed he'd hired Lydia Monroe. He was about to correct it, when she extended her hand to first Mr. Smith and then Mrs. White.

"I'm delighted to be here and I can't wait to meet your children."

"This is wonderful! I can't wait to tell the rest of the parents. I'm having a tea this afternoon, Miss Monroe. You must promise to come so I can introduce you to the other mothers."

"I'd like that Mrs. White."

Her fleshy face beamed in pleasure. "I live down at the far end of Elm Street. Drop by at two o'clock."

"Thank you, I will."

The two parents left the building happily discussing the start of the school year, while Alexander was left looking at Miss Monroe.

"How could you do that?"

"Do what?" Batting her long lashes at him, she was looking mighty, pleased with herself.

"Don't play innocent with me, Miss Monroe. You know exactly what I'm talking about. You just let those people think that you're going to be the new teacher."

Looking around the room and glancing out the open door, she laughed. "I don't see anyone else standing in line for an interview, do you?"

Of course she was right. "It doesn't make any difference. I'm the one doing the hiring, not your aunt."

"Look you'll agree that everyone in this town is anxious to get this school open, right?"

Nodding, he folded his arms across his chest, wondering where her thoughts were heading.

"And there really isn't anyone else who's come forward to take the job now is there?"

Shaking his head, he mouthed the word "no" and knew exactly where she was going. He also knew he was about to be backed into a corner and there wasn't a thing he could do about it.

"So then, are you going to hire me?"

Chapter Three

Lydia studied Mr. Judson's face. He didn't look too pleased about the developments of the last few minutes. She wasn't worried and thought that soon he would be just as happy as those two parents were about the new teacher.

Walking away from him, she inhaled the woody smells still left in the building. This was going to be where she would spend most of her time and her mind was already working at a furious pace deciding what needed to be done.

There was so much that had to be accomplished prior to opening the doors for the students of Surprise. There were primers that needed to be ordered and each child would need a journal to write his or her thoughts in. She thought back to her

25

school days, remembering what supplies were used by the boarding school teachers. There were writing tablets, pencils, and for the younger students, pieces of slate and bits of chalk.

Lydia intended to make every moment fun. She felt the excitement stirring inside of her. She was going to be responsible for shaping these young minds! No matter that she was inexperienced as a teacher; she and the children would learn together.

"I hope you're happy."

She spun around at the sound of his voice.

Summoning up her brightest smile, she faced him. "I am very happy as you should be, too."

Folding his arms across his chest, he looked down his nose at her. "Why should I be happy? You have successfully deceived two parents by letting them think that *you* are to be teaching their children."

Carefully, she took a step closer to him. "Do you have anyone else in mind for the job, Mr. Judson?"

She saw the fleeting look of doubt that crossed his face and knew even before he responded that he didn't. Tapping her foot impatiently she asked, "Well, do you?"

"No. But that doesn't mean that I approve of you."

"Of course not, I wouldn't expect you to." Though she tried not to feel hurt by his declaration and indeed she didn't want to desire his approval, Lydia hoped he could at least try to look pleased with the prospect of her as the new teacher. Instead, with his mouth stretched tight in a thin line and his brow furrowed, Mr. Judson looked as if he'd just swallowed a bitter pill.

No matter. If the school were to open in the next week, she had to go to the Mercantile and see to ordering the supplies. Lydia was too busy to fuss over this man's dark mood. About to leave to take care of business, Lydia felt his hand on her arm, pulling her to a stop.

"I hope we will not regret hiring you, Miss Monroe."

Leaning in close to him, so close she could see the dark flecks in his eyes—and something much more magnetic that would best be saved for later reflection—Lydia said, "There will be no regrets, Mr. Judson."

He released his hold on her as she pulled free; there was nothing more to say. Lydia walked out into the brilliant day, shielding her hand over her eyes; she headed to Main Street humming a little ditty.

By the time she reached Mr. Jules's store, Lydia had made mental notes of everything she needed for the school. Entering the store, she went straight to the back counter and hit the top of the bell with her hand, letting Mr. Jules know he had a customer.

"Ah, Miss Monroe, so good to see you. Are you here to buy some fabric, or perhaps I could interest you in the latest bonnets just in from a haberdasher in New York City?"

Tempting as his offer was, Lydia knew she needed to purchase the children's items first, then she could browse for herself. Smiling at him, she replied, "I'm here to get some supplies, Mr. Jules."

Pushing a tablet and pencil towards her, Mr. Jules raised his eyebrows. "May I inquire what these supplies might be for?"

"They're for the school. You see, I'm the new teacher." Taking the tablet, she began to list all the items, checking twice to be certain she hadn't forgotten anything. Satisfied that she'd listed everything, Lydia handed the tablet back to him.

"Pardon me for asking, but Miss Lydia, have you ever taught before?"

The nerve of the man to question her abilities! She should have noticed the doubtful look on the man's face sooner, but she'd been more intent on the task at hand than on observing the proprietor of the Mercantile.

Drawing herself up to her full height, she forced a smile. "I'll have you know that I've already met a few of the parents and they are simply delighted to have me as the teacher of their children."

Seeing that he'd hurt her feelings, Mr. Jules made every effort to make up for it. "Well, rightly so. You are, after all, Miss Margaret's niece and come from a very good family." Reaching across the counter he patted her hand. "Why don't you take a look at the new bolts of fabric while I see to your order?"

As tempting as his offer was, Lydia needed to go. "Thank you, Mr. Jules, but that will have to wait for another time."

She left the store and hurried across the street to the sheriff's office. Hopefully, Abigail wasn't too busy to see her. First Mr. Judson and then Mr. Jules with their doubtful airs, Lydia didn't know what to think. Maybe she had acted in haste when she'd given into her aunt's wishes.

Abigail would know what to do. The door to the office stood open, and Lydia walked in. Abigail was sitting behind her desk studying a pile of wanted posters. "Are you looking for my future husband?" Lydia laughed, referring to the fact that her cousin's husband was once featured on a wanted poster.

Of course they hadn't been married at the time. Cole had been wanted in connection with a robbery in Albany and he just happened to end up in Surprise at the same time Abigail had taken the post as sheriff.

"Lydia Louise!" Rounding the desk, Abigail

embraced her. "I doubt there will be anyone suitable for you in this batch of posters."

Lydia looked at her cousin. Abigail was blooming with happiness. Marriage and this job suited her well. "You look radiant, Abigail."

"Thank you. And you look worried."

"I was hoping not to be quite so obvious."

Closing the door to the office, Abigail turned to face her cousin. "Come, sit down and tell me what's going on."

Sitting in the small leather chair across from the desk, Lydia smoothed down her skirts trying to quiet the doubts swirling around her. "I'm going to be working at the schoolhouse when it opens in two weeks."

Of course she could have just come right out and said she'd be teaching, but then where was the fun in that? Better to let Abigail ask her.

"That's wonderful! What are you going to be doing?"

"Teaching," she blurted the word out.

She nodded, knowingly. "Aunt Margaret strikes again." Abigail shuffled and stacked the paperwork, then, folding her hands in front of her on the desk, looked at Lydia.

"So what did the school committee have to say about this?"

Shrugging, Lydia tried to appear nonchalant.

"I'm not sure about the rest of the members, but Alexander Judson isn't too pleased with the idea."

"Interesting."

"Why do you say that, Abigail?" Lydia wanted to know everything there was to know about the man who would serve as her superior.

"No reason. It's just that he's been so wrapped up in his business and caring for his children, I can't imagine he'd have the time to care about the teacher."

Scooting to the edge of her seat, Lydia replied, "Oh he cares, all right." She proceeded to tell Abigail what had transpired, finishing with, "the man doesn't seem to have any compassion. He's stubborn and condescending. I'm not sure I even like him all that much."

"Really."

"Yes, really." Lydia didn't like the look on her cousin's face. She was smiling in that knowing way, like she had some secret about the man.

"You know what they say about someone who protests too much?"

"No, I don't." Then it hit her. Lydia sprang from the chair, heading towards the door. "I am not attracted to him. I can't believe you'd even think such a thing!"

"Did I say anything at all to that effect, Lydia?"

Reaching for the door handle, she said, "You didn't have to, it's written all over your face." She left the office with the sound of Abigail's laughter ringing in her ears.

Lydia did not like the man. Admittedly he was handsome, but he was far too self-absorbed for her taste. Simply put, Alexander Judson wasn't her type.

The next week flew by as Lydia busily prepared for her first day of lessons. The books, tablets, and writing utensils arrived on Friday. Saturday and Sunday were spent making sure there were enough supplies for each student. By her calculations there would be twenty children attending. Of course, that number could very well climb once word got out about the new building being open.

She hoped so. "The more the merrier" was her motto.

After carefully studying the teaching guides, Lydia calculated that she had a month's lessons planned out. These included learning letters and numbers for the younger students, math, reading, and history for the older ones.

The next order of business was to decide on her wardrobe. After careful consideration, she decided against drab dark schoolmarmish colors with good reason—she didn't own any. So for the first day of classes, Lydia donned a blue and white calico day gown with a matching blue shawl, bonnet and gloves.

After patting her red hair, swept in a conservative French knot, and giving herself a final spritz of perfume, Lydia Louise Monroe set off for her first day of school.

The sight that greeted her almost made her turn tail and run back home to Aunt Margaret.

Chapter Four

"**R**obert! Laura!" Alexander was busy packing lunch buckets, tidying the cooking area, and still had to make the beds. His son and daughter were nowhere to be found. While he felt bad for Mrs. Sutherland, he wished she could have been sick on another day.

This was the first day of school and he wanted to be there to greet the parents, as well as the teacher. Time was wasting away.

His frustration growing, Alex yelled, "Robert and Laura, answer me right now!"

"We're on the porch, Papa." Robert poked his head inside the door. "Laura and I are ready to go."

Taking a deep breath, Alex made himself calm

down, knowing that taking his frustrations out on his children was unfair. Exhaling, he finished putting their lunches in the pails and gathered his things to join them.

He paused when he saw his daughter, so much the image of her mother. The same blue eyes and innocent smile looked up at him. Pain tugged at his heart. It was on days like these that he missed his wife the most. Joanna should be the one putting ribbons in Laura's hair and combing Robert's unruly curls into place, not him.

Today wasn't a day for dwelling on those thoughts, though. With great effort, he pushed his sorrow deep inside. Straightening his shoulders and taking a fortifying breath, he ushered them off the porch.

"Tell us about our teacher, Papa." Laura happily skipped along beside him.

What was there to say about the woman with the fiery red hair that would satisfy a child's curiosity. He couldn't very well tell them that Miss Monroe was highly unqualified, or that he'd been filled with doubts about the woman since he first laid eyes upon her.

Instead he opted for the easy way out. "She's a very kind woman." At least that was the truth. Alex felt she might very well have a kind heart and certainly would never harm any child.

"I hope she doesn't give a lot of homework," Robert scoffed.

He smiled down at his children, so typical in their concerns. Laura wanted someone who would be nice while Robert was only concerned about his playtime being taken over by after-school work.

As they neared the building, Laura placed her hand in his, moving closer will each step. He wanted to allay her fears. "I'm positive that you'll have a grand time. Look—there's Daisy Drumm. You like playing with Daisy, don't you, Laura?"

Her blonde head bobbed up and down.

"Maybe Miss Monroe will seat you next to her; that would be fine now wouldn't it?"

"Yes, Papa. Can I go talk to Daisy?"

"Run along." Releasing her hand, he smiled as the two girls caught each other in a hug. Robert had already gone off to join his group of friends. The outside yard was filled with parents and children all anxious to start the day.

Scanning the crowd, Alex was surprised he didn't see the teacher. He hoped she wasn't foolish enough to be tardy on the first day of classes. That wouldn't go over well with the committee, all of whom were there.

He was hailed by Mrs. Bartholomew, owner of the boarding house over on Low Road. "Mr. Judson, just look at all these happy faces!"

Happy faces, indeed. He thought the parents

wore the brightest smiles of the day. Several of the boys had already run off to play kick ball, including his son Robert, and the young girls stood in a circle giggling at their antics, oblivious to their parents's delight at being free of them for a few short hours.

"I hope the teacher arrives soon," was all he managed to get out before he noticed her making a path through the children. A hush fell over the crowd as children and parents alike turned to gaze at the new schoolteacher.

Miss Lydia Monroe was a sight to behold. The morning sunlight bounced off her vibrant red hair. Parents who hadn't had a chance to meet her before stared awestruck by her appearance. The pretty blue dress she wore wasn't exactly what Alex would call proper attire for the job; the fabric clinging to every curve of her body.

As he looked around at the expectant faces, he wondered if he was the only one to notice how out of place she looked. Sweet scents filled his nostrils. Just as he was looking for the source of the intoxicating smell, he found Lydia's gloved hand outstretched to his.

"Good morning, Mr. Judson. Isn't it wonderful the turnout we have for the first day of classes?"

Her smile was as brilliant as the color of her hair as she greeted him. The clearing of a throat from behind him reminded him how rude it would appear if he didn't accept her handshake.

Extending his hand towards hers, he said, "Yes. It is better than the committee could have hoped for. I assume you have everything in order." The scent belonged to her.

Something flashed in those green eyes right before she answered, "Of course."

Anger. Trepidation. He couldn't say for sure which, and it really didn't matter, for in the next minute she was climbing the four steps to the doorway. He admired the soft curves of her backside as she reached up, pulling on the leather cord, ringing the school bell.

A cheer went up from the townsfolk and with that the school was opened. Alex didn't know if he was relieved or frightened. He'd bet a week's worth of wages that that woman wouldn't last the month.

Turning away from the crowd, he walked over to his lumberyard. Cole was already waiting for him when he walked into the office.

"You looked worried," he said to Alex.

Grabbing the tin coffeepot off the coal stove, Alex poured himself a cup of the strong brew. "I suppose I shouldn't be. But I can't seem to help myself. You know as well as I do how flighty Lydia Monroe is."

His friend simply smiled.

"I don't even want to know what you're thinking," Alex said to his amused friend.

Cole said, "I'm thinking that I've almost finished the shelves for Jules over at the Mercantile."

Alex harrumphed.

"And Mr. White stopped by to ask about the lumber order for his house."

"To pester us, you mean. What'd you tell him?"

"I told him it would be ready by the end of the week."

Sipping his coffee thoughtfully, Alex swallowed and said, "We'll have it done by then." He gave one last glance toward the school and then settled in for a long day's work.

Lydia sat behind the big oak desk, carefully going over the first test of the school year. Though the students had groaned as if she were going to torture them, they'd set right to work once she explained it was just so she could place them in the proper groups for learning.

Taking advantage of the excitement that a new teacher could bring, she'd given them a short reading assignment to do while she corrected the papers. A snicker from the back of the room drew her attention.

Looking up she saw Robert Judson poke Clara White in the back. Clearing her throat, she caught his attention and shook her head. He quickly put his head back in the book. Lydia smiled. Her gaze scanning the room, she was happy to see all of her charges busy reading.

When she'd seen the crowd outside in the morning, she hadn't been sure what to expect. It felt as if suddenly the entire future of the town was resting on her shoulders. Unaccustomed to such feelings, Lydia had nearly gone back on her word to Aunt Margaret. But then there was Alexander Judson standing there with that look on his face, the one that said he doubted her abilities.

Rising to his silent challenge, Lydia decided she was going to prove him wrong in every way. It certainly wasn't her fault that the man was grouchy and miserable all of the time. Furthermore, there was no need for him to take his problems out on her. She saw the censure in his eyes when she'd arrived after everyone else this morning.

How was she supposed to know that the entire town would turn out early for the opening of the school? Mr. Judson had anticipated everyone arriving early. He could have tipped her off. But he didn't. She was thinking that maybe he wanted her to fail at this job.

Looking at the papers still needing to be corrected, Lydia realized time was ticking away while she lamented about the owner of the Lumber Company.

A few minutes later the children started to get

restless, so Lydia called a playtime. The children trooped outside and quickly broke off into groups. Laura Judson remained at her side.

Kneeling down so she was at Laura's height, Lydia looked into her sky blue eyes. "Is something the matter?"

The precious little girl shook her head, her blonde ringlets swaying. "No, Miss. Is it okay if I stay by you?"

"Wouldn't you rather play with your friends? I see Daisy Drumm over by the tree. She's waving at you. Go run along and play with her."

Laura moved closer to her. Lydia didn't know what to make of this. Laura hadn't seemed shy when she came to school this morning. She'd happily run along beside Daisy and Lydia had even sat them next to each other in the classroom. Still those big blue eyes were looking up at her unwaveringly.

Seeing that Laura wasn't going to budge, Lydia suggested, "Why don't we go over and visit with Daisy, would that be all right with you?"

"Yes, Miss."

Once the girls were together, Laura appeared to be fine, happily playing ring-around-the-rosy with several other girls her age. Lydia wondered about the little girl's need to be close to her. She hadn't had any contact with Laura except for today. It was amazing how quickly the girl had taken to her.

Lydia smiled; it felt good to be needed. Pulling her watch from her skirt pocket, she checked the time and saw the children only had five minutes of playtime left. The day was so beautiful though, it would be a shame to waste it indoors. Sunlight poured from the brilliant blue sky. A breeze kept the air at a comfortable temperature.

There was no reason why they couldn't continue their lessons right here in the yard. Clapping her hands together, she summoned her charges. "Come gather round, everyone."

When they'd all settled close to her, she moved to sit under the big oak tree where the girls had been playing. "What do you think about spending some more time outside?"

Cheers and laughter rang out. Lydia beamed. "Quiet down now, or we'll have to go back inside." When everyone had found a place to sit in the grass, Lydia looked at all the little shiny faces staring back at her expectantly.

"What would you like to work on first, letters or numbers?"

The children all began chattering at once. Finally Lydia raised her hand getting their attention. "Let's see a show of hands. How many would like to do letters?" She counted ten hands. "Now how many would like to do numbers?" Nine arms shot up.

"It looks like we're going to learn some letters."

Groans erupted from some of the boys who were clearly not happy with the outcome of the vote. "We'll work on our numbers after lunch."

Lydia spent the next hour teaching her students a song, and by lunchtime they'd all learned how to sing their letters. Sitting back against the tree, she listened with a keen ear as they started the second round of their ABC's. Nineteen voices blended together in a simple harmony.

The rest of the day passed quickly, and before she knew it, Lydia was ringing the bell dismissing them. The parents gathered up their youngsters and headed off. Only the Judson children remained. Lydia was fuming, how could Mr. Judson leave his children to be last the ones picked up? The man obviously gave them no thought whatsoever.

"Let me gather my things and we'll see about getting you home."

Laura looked up at her with tears brimming in her big round eyes. "Did my papa forget us?"

Robert stood beside his sister. "He has lots to do, Laura. Papa told us that last night, remember?"

She shook her head.

Fighting with her anger, she thought it unfortunate that this little boy had to make excuses for his father. Smiling down at the brother and sister, she offered, "I think I might have some cookies leftover from my lunch." Hurrying she went back to her desk and found her lunch pail, taking out the treat, she went back outside to find the two of them sitting on the top step with their chins resting on their hands.

Handing each of them a cookie, she said, "I'll just be a minute." All the while, Lydia was thinking that a cookie was a sad replacement for a father.

Leaving them to nibble away, Lydia went inside to gather her belongings. She wasn't inside for more than two minutes when she heard Laura's squeal. Dropping the papers she'd been putting in her satchel, she raced outside to see what was happening.

"Papa!" Laura launched herself into his arms.

Robert stayed where he was looking up at his father. Lydia stood framed in the doorway with her hands on her hips.

"Good afternoon, Mr. Judson."

"Afternoon, Miss Monroe." He tipped his hat to her.

"You're late."

"Sorry if I kept you waiting." Looking up at her, he offered a smile of apology.

The slow easy smile left his face when he noticed that she wasn't returning it. "Laura, why don't you and Robert start home, I'd like to have a word with Miss Monroe." Setting his daughter on the ground, he looked at Lydia.

Narrowing her eyes, she stared down at him.

Climbing two steps he stood at eye-level with her. Refusing to be intimidated by this man, Lydia stood her ground. Tension snapped around them like streaks of lightening as they continued their standoff.

He broke the silence. "I can see that you're upset with me. I'm sorry if my being late ruined the rest of your day."

"It's not my day that's been ruined, Mr. Judson. It's your children's."

Her comment seemed to grab his attention. Putting one foot up on the riser she was standing on, he glared at her. "May I remind you that your job is to teach, and not to scold parents who work hard all day in order to put food on their family's table!"

"There is no need for you to raise your voice." Lydia was barely containing her anger, but she at least had the good conscious not to make a scene. "Your children are waiting for you."

Looking over his shoulder, he noticed them waiting for him at the edge of the school yard. "Good day, Miss Monroe."

"Good day, Mr. Judson."

Chapter Five

The three cousins sat at the table flanking their aunt; it was weekly teatime. Aunt Margaret insisted that every Friday afternoon they all gather at her home to, as she put it, "catch up." This week was no different.

It was Maggie's turn to pour. "Lydia, I've been hearing some interesting comments about you."

Lydia could swear her heart rate just spiked. She'd been on edge since her last meeting with the unpleasant Alexander Judson. He was technically the one she answered to, and since she was growing surprisingly fond of her job, she didn't want to do anything to further displease him.

Carefully placing the delicate tea cup on the saucer, she looked at Maggie. "I hope they are at least helpful comments." She hadn't mentioned their exchange with anyone.

"Don't go fretting. I've heard glowing reports from the widow Sutherland," said her aunt.

"Aunt Margaret, she hardly counts. I mean after all, she doesn't have any children, leastwise not ones that I teach."

"Phooey! She cares for the Judsons while Alexander is working. I'd say that gives her the right to have a say about you." Aunt Margaret reached out to take a ginger cookie off one of the plates on the table. Nibbling thoughtfully, she turned her attention to Maggie.

Relieved to have the pressure taken off of her for the time being, Lydia turned to Maggie. Their aunt had a rather unsettling way of getting them to say things that most times none of them wanted to discuss.

"And what have you been doing with yourself this past week, Maggie?"

Glancing anxiously from Lydia to Abigail, Maggie looked like a cornered animal. "Nothing much really."

"Did you take a look at the old Grange Hall like I asked?"

"Yes, I went over yesterday."

"Well, what do you think about the space? Will it be suitable for my next project?"

Shrugging, Maggie looked to remain as noncommittal as possible. "There's a good chance it would work."

"That's it? A good chance is all you're going to give the building. Well I suppose it's better than nothing." Aunt Margaret settled back in her chair contemplating the answer. "I'll check back with you in a couple of weeks, and Margaret, by that time I expect to know one way or the other if you are going to take on the project."

Lydia knew that Margaret Monroe Sinclair could not be stopped once she got an idea going. Poor Maggie; it was looking as if she were going to be heading up the renovation and opening of the new dance hall. She was thinking that handling the school children seemed a much easier task.

"Now, Lydia back to the subject of the school."

Blanching under her aunt's piercing gaze, she said, "I thought we had finished discussing that?" Then quickly changing the subject, added, "I really need to see to my wardrobe. I'd love to find some time for a fitting. Now that I'm out everyday I feel the need for some new dresses."

Abigail responded with, "I heard that Mr. Jules received a shipment of new fabrics."

A delightful shiver of anticipation ran down her spine. Fabric shopping was a favorite pastime, one that she hadn't been able to fit in as of late. "I wonder if he's gotten in the latest catalog from

Burden's. You know I haven't seen a fashion circular in weeks!"

"Let's go see, right after we finish our tea." Maggie's suggestion, while not going over well with Aunt Margaret, suited the cousins just fine. Within an hour they were riding off to town in the buggy.

It was a glorious day, the sunlight reflecting off the glacier-carved crevices of the Catskill Mountains in the distance. The sight of the peaks brought to mind the story of Rip Van Winkle. It was said that he wandered from town to town spreading good cheer. Lydia thought she'd have to find a way to work the folklore into a lesson.

"Maggie, looks to me like Aunt Margaret is going to make you her next project." It was Abigail who broached the topic of the new dance hall.

"Lord, I hope not. I left enough interfering family members to come here and be with you and Lydia. I was hoping those days were behind me."

Lydia could sympathize with her cousin's sentiments; she'd come here hoping to change some things in her life, too.

"You have to admit, Maggie that a dance hall would spice things up in Surprise. Let's face it, there really isn't much to do after dark here," Lydia chimed in.

"I suppose. I would, however, like to build the

business at my pace, not on Aunt Margaret's whim."

Lydia smiled. Dear Maggie was the sensible one. Where Maggie was concerned things had to be just so. As for herself, Lydia preferred to let the wind carry her. And that was the way she hoped to run her classroom—cheerful and worry-free.

Lately she'd had the constant feeling that she was being watched. The sensation had struck her twice in the past week, both times as she'd just been finishing up the day's lessons with the children. She supposed it could be her imagination, but if it happened again she was going to speak to Abigail about it.

Abigail pulled the buggy to a stop in front of The Mercantile. "Here we are, ladies. Let's go see what Mr. Jules has for us to look at today!"

The three women filed into the store with one mission in mind—shopping. Lydia felt her heart race in anticipation. She was hoping to find some yellow fabric for a new dress.

"Afternoon, ladies. Might I say you are all looking mighty pretty this afternoon," Cole Stanton drawled, dropping his hammer to take his wife in his arms.

"We do so thank you for the compliment, Cole. It's nice to see you," Maggie said. First Maggie and then Lydia greeted him with a kiss on his cheek.

Stepping out of his embrace, Abigail looked at his handiwork. "The shelves look nice."

"With all you ladies in town, Mr. Jules saw the need to do a little expanding to accommodate your tastes." Cole winked.

"I hardly think he did it just for us." Abigail shot back at him.

Wiggling his eyebrows at his wife, Cole said, "Oh, yes he did."

Playfully she slapped him on the arm. "You can stop teasing us now."

"I have to get back to work, ladies. Alexander wants this project finished today."

Lydia got the idea that Cole's boss was quite the taskmaster. Pushing thoughts of the man aside, she set her sights on some silks that she hadn't noticed the last time she was in the store. Removing her gloves, Lydia ran her hands over the smooth material. This would make a beautiful day gown, one she'd be able to wear to teach and would be suitable for dinner at home.

Calculating how much fabric would be needed, she began to search for ribbons and buttons to adorn the gown.

Behind her, the door to the shop opened and creaked shut. "Maggie, what do you think of this color?" Turning around with a swatch of yellow fabric held against her, Lydia was expecting Maggie to answer.

"Shouldn't you be at the schoolhouse working on next week's lessons, Miss Monroe?"

Flustered, she stared up at Mr. Judson. "I do get time off. I didn't think you'd expect me to be working twenty-four hours a day like you do Cole." She could have bitten her tongue off. It wasn't her business how many hours Cole worked. She knew from Abigail, though, that he was hardly ever home.

Leaning against the doorjamb, grinning, Alexander studied her in that unnerving way he had. "You could learn a thing or two about work ethics from the man."

"I don't know what you are talking about."

"I'm speaking of the way the children are allowed to run hither and yon when they are supposed to be inside learning."

So he was the one who'd been watching her. "Children can absorb more when they are allowed some freedom, Mr. Judson."

"And just where did you hear that one?"

"I . . . well, I . . ." she hated to be cornered in this way. It wasn't so much that she'd heard this, it was more in the way she instinctively knew how to get the best from her students. And keeping them cooped up in a stuffy room all day long was not the way to get results.

"You've been watching me."

He laughed. The man had the audacity to throw his head back and laugh at her! Recovering his wits, Alexander grinned at her. "I don't have to watch you, Miss Lydia, there are plenty of parents who come into town on made-up errands, just to check up on you."

"How dare they? How dare you! I'll have you know that I'm doing a fine job and no one, *no one* will tell you differently." Throwing the fabric back on the table, Lydia stormed outside.

Inhaling deeply, she fought to calm her temper. That man continually brought out the worst in her. He should be more concerned about raising his children than about her. The door open and closed behind her. Turning, she expected to find one of her cousins standing there, instead there stood Mr. Judson.

Lydia moved closer to the porch railing, allowing him room to pass by. When he didn't, she faced him, better to settle their differences right here and now.

"Why have you made it your business to hound me?"

"Need I remind you that I'm the one who will be in trouble if you don't succeed at your job?"

"I don't need any reminding, Mr. Judson. You are constantly around throwing your authority in my face." Hating confrontation, Lydia willed herself to remain calm, while at the same time wondering why the two of them just couldn't try and get along, for the sake of the children if nothing else.

"It's too bad you don't give this much attention to your own family," Lydia mumbled.

Taking a step closer to her, Alexander said, "I'm sorry, I didn't catch that remark."

"I said, don't you have work that needs tending to," she lied.

Frowning he looked towards his lumber company. The buzzing of the saws echoed in the air. "I suppose I do, but you and I have issues that need to be resolved."

Anger simmering once more. Lydia folded her arms in front of her and turned her back to him. She wasn't going to waste anymore of her time bantering with this man. Perhaps after ignoring him for a few minutes he'd get the hint and return to his business.

"Look, I think we should at least try to get along, don't you?" She decided to try to put an end to their childish rivalry.

Lydia slowly turned to look at him, and was surprised by the change in his manner. There was actually a bit of a smile playing about his mouth. Puckering her mouth, she continued to study him. His dark eyes showed none of the animosity that had been there a few moments before.

Thinking that it wouldn't be a bad idea to do as he suggested, while at the same time wondering about this sudden change of heart, Lydia held out her hand. "Truce?"

Chapter Six

Taking her hand in his, he squeezed it gently. "Truce."

Suddenly unsure of himself, Alex released his hold on her. He noticed Lydia was studying him. With her head cocked to one side, he imagined she was trying to read his thoughts. Smiling, he knew she'd be mighty surprised if she knew what was going on inside of his head while the sweet scent of her perfume swirled around them, holding his senses hostage.

He hadn't realized until this very moment how much he'd missed being around a woman. But Lydia Louise Monroe certainly wasn't his type. She was too much like a bumble bee flitting from one flower to the next in search of just the right nectar.

Clearing her throat nervously, Lydia interrupted his thoughts. "I should be going back inside to finish with my purchases."

Tipping his hat to her, Alexander stepped aside, allowing her to pass by. "I'll be seeing you around, Miss Monroe."

She was just about to enter the store, when she stopped and looking over her shoulder at him, smiled. "Yes, I'm sure we'll be running into each other soon."

In the next instant she was inside and Alex was left feeling like a schoolboy fawning after his first crush. Shuddering at the thought, he began walking in the direction of the lumberyard.

When he'd first entered the store and saw her standing there holding the fabric against her, he'd been intent on goading her for he still saw her as nothing more than another one of Miss Margaret's overindulged nieces. After he'd spoken, though, the distress shown so clearly on her face made him feel like a complete heel.

Even worse, Miss Monroe was the one who'd extended the proverbial olive branch, calling a truce. He'd no choice except to take her up on the offer of at least trying to get along. It surprised him to realize what little effort had been required to do so.

Whistling a simple tune, he walked into the dim interior of his building. If nothing else was right in his life, at least he'd managed to build a very successful business here in Surprise. Judson Lumber Company was something he was proud of and was a legacy that he would be able to leave his son and daughter.

Closing the door to his office, Alex sat down behind his desk and concentrated on prioritizing the orders that had been streaming in for the past month. He'd been working for two hours when Cole returned.

Entering the office, Cole sat in the chair opposite the desk. Tossing his hat on the desk, he looked at Alex.

Alex's first thought was that something had gone wrong with one of their projects. Bracing himself for the report, he asked, cautiously, "What's wrong?"

"We've know each other for how long now, Alex?"

With a quick shrug, he replied, wondering the reason for the question, "I don't know, the better part of a year, I suppose."

"That's about right. And in all that time you never once judged me." Grinning, he added, "regardless of what the feelings of the townsfolk were."

He knew Cole was referring to the time he'd spent mistakenly locked up in the local jail. "Yes. I'm not sure where you're heading with this, Cole."

Leaning forward, Cole rested his elbows on his knees. "Well now, let me tell you where I'm going. You see, Miss Lydia was right upset with how you treated her earlier, and seeing how I'm married to her cousin and a part of the family, I think it's my responsibility to tell you when you're crossing the line to rudeness."

Alex felt his temper rise. "I think that's between me and Miss Monroe."

"Not when you conduct yourself so poorly in a public place."

"Cole, you know I value your friendship, but . . ."

"Then you will understand what I'm about to say is for your own good." Cole cut him off. "I know that you've suffered a great loss in your life. And from what I hear, before that you weren't such a hardened man. You have two beautiful children and a lifetime still ahead of you."

"My personal life is none of your business!" His clenched fist landed on the desk with a loud thud.

The silence hung in the air like so many dust

motes. He would never admit that Cole's comments struck him to the very core of his soul.

Cole didn't back down. "I'm sorry, Alex, but you made it my business when you started treating Lydia so poorly. It's one thing to comment on her abilities as a teacher when she's in the classroom, but to insult her the way you just did at The Mercantile is unacceptable."

Had he truly been so busy hardening his heart over the past two years that he'd forgotten how to act and feel? How could he have completely lost all sense of manners when it came to dealing with women, especially with one Miss Lydia Monroe? Closing his eyes, he took a deep breath. He was acting like a complete buffoon.

"Maybe if she was a little more stable I wouldn't have such trouble dealing with her."

"She's not like that all the time. From what I've seen Lydia really loves teaching the children. She's taken quite a liking to your two."

"Well, Robert and Laura are easy to love."

"I know. It's their father who worries me." Standing, Cole retrieved his hat from the desk. "Don't let life pass you by. Don't let this opportunity with Lydia pass you by."

"I hardly know the woman."

Walking to the door, Cole tossed over his shoulder, "Well, my friend, maybe it's time you got to know her."

Alex spent the rest of the day pondering Cole's last comment. He wasn't even sure he wanted to start a relationship with a woman, though there were times when he longed to feel the softness of a woman in his arms. Just a simple hug or someone waiting with a warm meal and a smile at the end of a long day would suffice.

He knew that eventually he'd want more than that. Right now his children needed more than he was able to give. While Mrs. Sutherland was a help, they all needed more in their lives than what the kindly older widow was providing.

In theory those thoughts were good, but what he didn't know was how to proceed—how to move on with his life.

With their purchases tucked away underneath the seat of the buggy, the Monroe cousins made their way back to Aunt Margaret's house.

"What on earth were you and Mr. Judson discussing?" Maggie questioned Lydia.

"Nothing."

"Well, I dare say, it looked like it was more than just 'nothing' that kept the two of you on the porch for so long," Abigail commented.

At the moment, Lydia didn't feel like defending herself to her cousins. She wanted to mull over what had just happened between her and one mighty handsome mill owner.

It seemed to her that there wasn't a thing she could do that Mr. Judson approved of. But then while they were on the walkway he almost looked like he might be coming around. She'd caught the fleeting look in those big brown eyes of his. It was a look she'd seen a hundred times in other men.

Except in Alexander's eyes she'd seen something more than just a fun flirtation. A part of her wanted to shout in triumph, but it was the other part of her, the part that knew he'd already had his heart broken, that made her take stock. She wondered what he'd been like before his wife's death. Had he always taken life so seriously? Now that the thought had entered her head, Lydia couldn't seem to move beyond it.

Somehow she knew that Alexander Judson was not a man who toyed with anyone's feelings, therefore she shouldn't be coy with his. She'd do well to remember this. For as far back as Lydia could remember, she'd been in the habit of taking relationships with the opposite sex lightly, never falling in love with any man.

Her life was too short to commit to only one person. That was how she felt before she'd met Alexander Judson. And now . . . now her feelings were turned upside down and she didn't know what to do.

Chapter Seven

The following week Mrs. Sutherland came down with a bad cold and Alexander ordered her to stay home until she felt better. With the children and his business to look after, he found himself stretched to the limit. The first day hadn't been a problem for him. Managing to get them off to school and be there at the end of the day to pick them up was less of a hassle than he'd expected.

The second day he found himself in a quandary. Cole had taken the wagon into Catskill for some supplies so Alexander was left without anyone to take over for him when Laura and Robert were finished with school.

At noon he went over to the schoolyard. It didn't take him long to spot Miss Lydia. With her red hair tied back in a ponytail she sat underneath a big oak tree with a group of children surrounding her. His daughter Laura was sitting on her right side while her 'very best friend in the whole world', or so she'd informed him just this morning, Daisy Drumm, sat to the left.

Smiling when he heard their giggling, Alex slowed his step, taking in the scene. He felt his heart softening a little more towards the teacher. In a short time she'd managed to brighten his children's lives, as well as those of the rest of the town. For that he would be forever grateful.

She looked up when she heard his approach. Rising quickly she brushed her green skirt into order.

"Mr. Judson. Good afternoon."

Doffing his hat, he nodded. "Afternoon."

Spotting him, Laura launched herself into his arms. "Papa! Miss Lydia was telling us a story about Rip Van Winkle."

Hugging his daughter close, he inhaled the sweet, innocent scent of her. "Mmmm. Rip Van Winkle, huh."

Nodding her head excitedly, Laura said, "He fell asleep right here in our mountains. Did you know that, Papa? Have you ever seen him?"

"I may have heard a story or two about old Rip, but I've never run across the man." Turning his attention to the teacher, he asked with a wink,

"What about you, ma'am, have you ever met the man?"

"Surely I have not. I daresay it would be difficult to find him, considering how it is rumored that he traveled from town to town never staying in one place for very long."

"Yes, well then, it makes sense that no one has ever met the man." Setting Laura down on the ground, he watched as she and Daisy ran off hand-in-hand to play on the teeter-totter.

Following the direction of his gaze, Lydia said, "Laura has certainly come out of her shell."

"Yes, she has and I owe that all to you, Miss Monroe."

Her lips twitched as she turned her green-eyed gaze to look at him. "Thank you for the compliment. Although I think being around other children had more to do with her change."

"Maybe."

"So what brings you here on such a fine afternoon?" Shielding her eyes from the noonday sun, she scanned the area, checking on all of the children.

"I know what you're thinking."

Not taking her eyes off her charges, she inquired, "And what might that be?"

"That I'm here to check up on you."

Dropping her hand to her side, she gave him her full attention. "Are you?"

"No, I'm not." And that, he realized, was the God's honest truth. For the most part, everyone in town was pleased with her performance. There was still the issue of her unorthodox teaching methods, but he wasn't here to discuss those with her.

Continuing to study him with those green eyes, she made him uneasy. Getting right to the point would probably be the best thing for him to do right now.

"Actually, I came to ask a favor."

"Really?" She smiled up at him.

"Yes, really. Mrs. Sutherland is under the weather and I've had to send Cole out of town on an errand that won't bring him back until after supper time." Suddenly he felt nervous. What made him think she would help him? After all he hadn't been very cordial to her when she'd first arrived.

"I don't see what this has to do with me."

"I need someone to watch my children." He hadn't meant to blurt it out in such a manner, but the woman was making him downright nervous with her penetrating stare.

"And you think that I might know of someone to fill in until she gets better?"

"I was hoping you could walk Robert and Laura home this afternoon and stay with them until I can leave work."

With her eyebrows raised in surprise, Lydia continued to stare at him, only this time her smile widened into a grin. "I must admit, Mr. Judson, I'm quite flattered that you consider me competent enough to take care of your children."

Her comment ruffled his feathers. "Of course you're competent."

Anger flashed in her eyes causing him to quickly amend his statement. "I was hoping it wouldn't be too much trouble. Laura and Robert like you. I could have them come join me at work, but I don't like to have them around the saws when they are running."

Sensing her lingering doubt, he added with what he hoped was a warm smile, "I'll be home at six o'clock sharp."

"That will be fine, Mr. Judson. We shall see you at dinner time."

With that she walked off and left him standing still holding his hat in hand, while she rang the bell at the top of the steps, signaling the end of lunchtime.

By the time she rang the school bell again, Lydia had to admit to feeling a tad nervous about agreeing to help Mr. Judson. Before their last lesson, she'd told Robert and Laura that she would be taking them home. The children had been delighted with the news.

Lydia, on the other hand, was beginning to realize just how needy the Judson children were.

Gathering up the papers she'd be correcting this evening, she went to find them.

"Robert, Laura!" She called out to them, waiting at the edge of the yard while they caught up with her.

"Miss Lydia, I'm glad you're taking us home today."

"Why thank you, Laura." The little girl tucked her hand inside of Lydia's.

"You aren't going to make us do any homework are you?" Robert asked, scuffing his feet in the dirt. It was clear that he wasn't too pleased about his teacher taking him home.

"Now how often have I sent you home with extra work?"

"Just that one time, Miss Lydia."

"That's right, and it was only because you needed to practice your letters."

Satisfied that he wasn't going to be spending the rest of the day doing homework, he skipped on ahead of Lydia and Laura. By the time they reached the house, Robert had already changed out of his school clothes.

Eager to please, he stood on the porch with a small tin bucket in his hands. "I'm going to collect the eggs."

"It's my turn to get the eggs!" Releasing her hold on Lydia's hand, she ran off after her brother.

Unsure of the trouble they could get into in the

small barn, Lydia hastily followed. It didn't take long for the flock of a dozen or so chickens to realize they had company. The red hens gathered around their feet, pecking along the dirt and even at the tips of Lydia's shoes.

Shooing them away, she entered the low-ceiled shed where the chickens were housed. Robert was reaching into one of four layer boxes and Laura was rushing ahead of him trying to beat him to the next one when the pail came crashing to the ground.

Yellow yolks oozed out of the cracked brown shells coating the ground in a thin slimy film.

"Look what you did, Laura!" Robert shouted at his sister in disgust.

"It was an accident. I . . . didn't mean . . . to do it," she managed to hiccup the words as big fat tears rolled down her chubby cheeks.

Never having been left alone with children of any age, with the exception of her students, Lydia was at a loss as to how she should go about handling this situation. The eggs were clearly ruined and she fervently hoped they didn't need them for supper.

Laura's cries soon turned to wails and Robert decided to assert his authority as the oldest by standing over her with hands fisted on his hips. "Pa isn't going to be happy about this mess."

"He won't care . . ."

Even though the words were spoken defiantly, Lydia could see the fear making its way into the little girl's eyes.

"All right now, let's just clean up this mess and then you can show me your home." No sooner had the words come out then the flock of chickens, sensing a meal, came running into the shed scratching and pecking at the broken eggs like it was their last meal.

The unexpected sight of this made Lydia erupt in laughter. Soon Robert and Laura were giggling at the birds' antics, too.

"I guess we don't have to worry about the mess after all, do we?"

"No, Miss Lydia. The hens like to eat the broken eggs. They like to eat everything. You should see them go after our dinner scrapings."

Leading them back to the house, she said, "I expect it is a sight to behold."

"Maybe tonight you can stay for supper and then you can see for yourself how they are."

The comment gave Lydia pause. There hadn't been any invitation to dinner extended by their father; which reminded her that she'd no idea how to prepare a meal. Anna always cooked up at Aunt Margaret's house, and back home her mother had a girl who came by during the day to clean and cook.

Hopefully she wouldn't have to worry about

cooking, for surely Mr. Judson would be home long before the children needed to be fed.

These dire thoughts were interrupted by Laura. "Come inside, Miss Lydia."

Lydia took in the humble household as she stepped across the threshold. The entry gave way to a large keeping room where the kitchen and dining area were combined. Through a large doorway she could see a small parlor.

Taking hold of her hand, Laura guided her through the house. Pointing out a large overstuffed chair angled towards the fireplace, she said, "This is where Papa reads us stories."

Down a short hallway were two doors, one on the left and one on the right. Tugging her along, Laura pushed open the door on the right side. "This is Robert's and my room."

Two single beds lined either side of the wall, a small window separating them. Robert's bed was covered in a blue and white patchwork quilt, while his sister's bore a matching design in pink. There was a small four drawer built-in dresser. The walls were white-washed and the planked flooring had a blue and white rag rug covering a portion of it.

Stuffed bears and dolls lined the shelf along one wall. All in all, Lydia thought it was a nice room for the children. Before she could stop her, Laura was pulling her in to the opposite room. The starkness was shocking.

There weren't any colorful quilts in here instead the double bed looked barely slept in. As if reading her thoughts, Robert explained. "Papa falls asleep in the big chair."

Assuming he meant the one she'd be shown earlier, Lydia wondered that Alexander Judson was always in such a sour mood. Looking about the rest of this bedroom she saw plain unadorned walls. Her gaze fixed on a small night stand with a kerosene lantern and a picture frame. Daring to step closer she studied the portrait.

It was of a woman. She had Laura's blue eyes and Robert's smile. Alexander's wife; their mother. Knowing what she knew now; the fact that the man couldn't bear to sleep in this room was a testament to how much he'd loved this woman.

The thought gave her pause. In all her harmless flirtations over the past few years Lydia had never felt anything close to what this man so clearly felt for his wife. She couldn't help wondering what his feelings were now.

"Miss Lydia, I'm hungry." Robert's plaintive cry drew her back to the reason she was here; to take care of these children.

Chapter Eight

Going back to the kitchen, Lydia found a jar of oatmeal cookies. Unscrewing the lid, she took out one for each of them and then poured the fresh milk from the pitcher that Robert handed her into three glasses.

"Mrs. Sutherland always leaves us a treat," he explained.

Lydia suspected no matter how kindly Mrs. Sutherland was, she was no substitute for a mother.

"I hope she feels better soon," he said between bites.

"I think she'll be on the mend before you know it," Lydia assured him.

"Can we play outside?" Laura gulped down her

last bit of milk and put the empty glass on the table.

Nodding, Lydia finished the snack and then gathering up the papers she'd brought with her, followed them outside. She sat in the slat-back rocker on the porch and began to rock gently. Before long the sounds of laughter and clucking chickens had her feeling quite content.

Seeing that the children were safe, playing on a swing hanging from a tree nearby, Lydia turned her attention to correcting the papers. It seemed as if she'd just started when they were at her feet asking when dinner would be ready.

"We just ate!" she chided softly.

"Mrs. Sutherland always cooks for us at this time."

Lydia had to bite her lip to keep from saying that she wasn't Mrs. Sutherland. She left them to play while she wandered slowly into the kitchen. What on earth could she possibly find to feed them?

Of course she could always give them another cookie to hold them over until their father came home. Or she could take the easy way out and bring them to Aunt Margaret's where Anna was sure to have enough for two extra mouths.

Just as she was thinking the latter idea would be best solution, she found a cloth-covered serving dish. Dear, sweet Mrs. Sutherland—even though she was sick the woman had managed to see to the evening meal.

Next to the chicken casserole sat a loaf of freshly baked bread. Lydia quickly busied herself setting the table. Unsure when Alexander would be home, she held his place setting off to one side. When the table was set for two and the casserole warmed, she sliced up some bread and called the children in to wash up.

By the time they were seated at the table the clock on the mantle was chiming six times. Anxiously, Lydia served up the dinner and then walking to the window pulled back the curtains, peering out into the dusk.

"Papa should be along at any minute," Laura reassured her.

The only thing Lydia saw were the glow of kerosene lamps in the windows of two houses off in the distance. No sign of Mr. Judson. Trying to keep her temper in check, she wondered at the audacity of the man. Clearly his children came second to his job.

Dropping the curtain back into place, she pasted a smile on her face and wandered back to the table where Robert and Laura were finishing their meal.

"It looks to me like Mrs. Sutherland is a good cook." Pulling out one of the two remaining chairs, she was about to sit when Robert said, "That's ma's place."

"She can sit there," Laura said softly. "Papa won't mind."

Uncertainty flooded through her. It saddened her to think that they were still mourning the loss of their mother after all these months. Lydia had never been in a situation like this before and she didn't know what to do.

Finally, after several moments of silence, she said, "I'll just sit in your papa's place, if that's all right?"

Sitting down, she thought about this family. How could Robert and Laura be expected to move on? Their father obviously didn't sleep in the bed he'd shared with his wife and kept an empty place at the table for her.

A youngster learned by example, and as far as Lydia could tell Mr. Judson was setting a pretty poor one. Clearly he'd loved his wife very much, but she was gone and in her mind it was beyond time for him to start enjoying life again.

"We're finished. May we be excused, Miss Lydia?"

Looking at Robert, she realized she'd stopped paying attention to them. "That would be fine. Can you get yourselves ready for bed?"

"It's hardly dark yet," he complained.

A bit of bribery wasn't beneath her. "If you get into your nightclothes then I can read you a story."

As they clambered off to their room, Lydia cleared the table. If Alexander didn't return within the next hour she would wash the dishes and leave him with a clean kitchen. Although not very domestic, she felt certain that she could handle this one small task. She'd gotten the dinner on the table without much fuss, hadn't she?

"We're ready!"

Turning at the sound of Laura's voice, she wiped her hands on a towel and crossed the room to the big overstuffed chair. It crossed her mind that this was the same one Mr. Judson slept in.

She sat down, making a space for Laura on her lap. The first thing that struck her was the scent of the cushions. It smelled of pine soap—masculine, like Alexander. A warm shiver raced down her spine, the reaction surprising her. Deliberately ignoring the feeling, she opened the pages of the storybook and began to read.

By the time the last page was turned, both children were stifling yawns. The clock on the mantle struck eight times. Where was he?

Ushering the children down the hallway, she heard Laura say to her brother, "Papa is busy again."

Did this mean that Mrs. Sutherland was the one who tucked them in at night? Was she the person who fed them their supper and read them their bedtime story? Lydia's heart ached for them.

"Come on, hop into bed and I'll listen to your nighttime prayers." Lydia sat on the edge of Laura's bed and pulled the blankets up to her chin.

"God Bless Papa, and Mrs. Sutherland. And keep Mama safe. Oh and I almost forgot, thank you for sending Miss Lydia for our teacher."

Lydia thought her heart might burst. Precious words from a precious darling little girl. Leaning down, she kissed Laura's forehead. "I'll see you in school bright and early."

"You don't need to tuck me in. And I already said my prayers to myself." Robert gripped the edges of his blanket with a look of fear on his face.

Realizing that he was afraid she was going to kiss him, and that he would never live it down if his friends found out, Lydia said a quick good night and left the room.

She had just started to worry about Alexander's lateness again when she heard the sound of light footsteps on the porch. She rushed to the door, threw it open, and demanded, "Where have you been?"

He laughed, a clear rich sound that infuriated her. "I don't see what's so funny, Mr. Judson."

Brushing past her, he entered his home. Taking off his jacket he hung it on the hook behind the door.

"Miss Monroe, it's been a very long time since

anyone has met me at my front door." Giving a shrug, he added, "You took me by surprise is all."

Tapping her foot and folding her arms in front of her, she said, "You are late."

Walking to the kitchen, he lifted the lid on the casserole. "I'm sorry. Cole got back much later than I'd expected." Bringing the dish to the table he asked, "Did you eat?"

She shook her head, realizing she was hungry.

Taking a plate from the drying rack, he set a place for her at the opposite end of the table; across from him in that place that his wife had occupied.

Lydia noticed the hesitation in Alexander, but didn't say a word. A soft sigh escaped him as he looked up, catching her staring at him.

Smiling at Lydia, he said, "I'll serve up the chicken and you can slice the bread."

The ease with which he ordered her about had her rooted to the spot.

Pausing with the serving spoon in hand, he quirked an eyebrow at her. "Let me guess, you don't know how to slice bread?"

Anger spurring her into action, Lydia strode to the table. Grabbing up the knife in one hand while squeezing the life out of the loaf with the other, she whacked off a crooked hunk of bread. Watching him in satisfaction, she did the same thing a second time. Only this time it was followed by a sharp, slicing pain through her index finger.

Blood oozed from the cut, soaking through the bread. "Yuck." It was a word she'd heard her students use many a time and had scolded them for it. But now seemed as appropriate a time as any for her to be using it.

"Geesh! You should have told me you couldn't handle the knife. I would have cut the bread." Alex rushed around to the other side of the table. Grabbing hold of her hand, he applied pressure to her finger stemming the flow of blood.

"I can handle a knife just fine, Mr. Judson. The handle was slippery is all."

He felt a tremble go through her and wondered if she were the crying type. Since he wasn't sure, Alex rushed her over to the sink. Grabbing the pump handle, he began to pump furiously bringing up cold well water.

When he could manage a good look at the cut, he saw it wasn't too deep. "This doesn't look too bad to me."

A small gash of a quarter-inch wide angled across her finger. "Keep some pressure on it." When he was certain she could do that, he released his hold and rummaged around on the counter until he found a clean cloth. Tearing a thin strip from it, he bandaged her finger.

"There. That should help."

"Thank you."

She'd turned away from the sink and was facing him. He very nearly was holding her in his arms. The feeling of having a woman in his arms had become so foreign that Alex wasn't sure what to do next. The only thing he knew was how good it felt to have her standing next to him.

Lydia was looking up at him with those green eyes, bewitching him. It was the only way to explain what happened next. Tipping his head he touched his mouth to her lips—lips that felt so soft and tasted so sweet.

He felt her remain still, and then, tentatively, return his kiss, moving her lips ever so slowly against his. It was as if they were frozen in time. For just these few brief moments he allowed himself to forget that he had responsibilities—and to forget that he'd had a wife whom he'd loved very much.

Deepening the kiss, Alexander became lost in the sense of all that was Lydia Louise Monroe. And then she broke it off. Looking into her eyes he saw doubts, questioning, and just a little excitement. A rosy flush spread across her cheeks.

"Alexander?"

His name spoken in a question gave him pause— left him wondering about what they'd just done.

Taking a quick step back, Alex swallowed hard. "I apologize for my boldness."

She opened her mouth as if to say something, but no words came out. Blinking, she looked down at the cut on her finger. "Thank you for the bandage. I think the bleeding has stopped." No mention of the kiss they shared.

Sighing, he raked a hand through his hair in frustration. What was he doing kissing *the schoolteacher* anyway? Turning away from her, he stared at the table where their now cold supper sat. His gaze drifting to the place where his wife sat for so many years; it was time to let go. He could feel it clear to his soul.

Turning to look at Lydia, he was about to apologize once more when the sound of an approaching wagon broke through the silence.

"Are you expecting someone?"

"Cole offered to drive you home. I didn't want you walking in the dark alone. I didn't think you'd mind."

"Thank you for thinking of my safety."

She bustled about the room, gathering her papers and shawl. Opening the door she gave him a quick glance over her shoulder and then was gone into the night.

Swearing softly, Alexander cleared away the dishes, leaving the casserole for the chickens. He'd lost his appetite. Then he walked down the short hallway opening the first door he came to. In the dim moonlight he could make out the forms of his sleeping children. He wondered what it had been like for them having a woman other than Mrs. Sutherland reading them their bedtime story and tucking them in for the night. Making them feel loved, cared for, safe.

Telling himself it hadn't made any difference, he closed the door and crossed the hallway, entering the room he'd once shared with his wife. Wearily, he sat on the edge of the double bed. Reaching out he took the picture off the nightstand and stared at it.

"Joanna." Whispering her name into the darkness, Alex felt the familiar pain of his loss rolling through him. Two long years had passed since her death and still he felt the sharp, stabbing pain.

Burying himself in his work had been the only way he could survive, that and taking care of his children. Though there were days when even their mere presence served as a painful reminder of what he'd lost.

His wife wasn't coming back. Perhaps it was time to finally move on. Surely Joanna wouldn't begrudge him happiness? Of course he knew deep down in his soul that she wouldn't want his children to remain motherless, just like she wouldn't want him to be alone for the rest of his life.

His wife had been a caring, unselfish person, it

was the thing that had attracted him to her in the first place—it was what had made losing her so unbearable.

He put the picture frame back on the nightstand, stood, and walked out the bedroom door. Within minutes he'd taken off his shoes, loosened his shirt collar and was sitting in the overstuffed chair in front of the cold fireplace.

Closing his eyes, Alexander willed sleep to claim him. Instead, visions of a certain red-headed green-eyed teacher filled his mind.

Chapter Nine

"Well, John, I think it's nigh on time that the good people of this town got to see the progress the children are making under the tutelage of my niece." Margaret was glad to have her friend and advisor here. John Wagner had been a great help in bringing Cole and Abigail together.

Margaret didn't know what she'd do without him. John had been by her side since her husband's death many years ago.

Quirking his eyebrows at her, he asked, "And just what are you suggesting, Miss Margaret?"

"Why an open house of course."

Chuckling at her predictability, John gave the expected argument. "Of course. Perhaps Lydia has already thought of this idea, she may even be planning it as we speak."

Shaking her head, she said, "No. Lydia's thoughts are filled with only one thing or should I say one person. Alexander Judson. Ever since she came back from his house the other night she's been acting strange. She hardly said a word at breakfast this morning."

Strumming her fingers on the arm of the chair, she pondered the situation. "Something is going on between those two."

John picked up a scone from the plate on the table sitting between them, and took a healthy bite. Swallowing the delectable morsels, he asked, "So you approve of this?"

"I do."

Margaret glanced out the window. It was another crystal-clear mountain morning. The town was growing beyond her wildest dreams. The near constant buzzing of the saws at the mill was proof Surprise was beginning to prosper again; just as she promised her dearly departed husband.

Rising from the chair, John said, "I must be getting back to the office."

"Have a good day and I'll let you know when the open house will be scheduled."

Smiling at his dear friend, he shook his head. "You don't give up do you, Margaret?"

"Why would I?"

"Why, indeed."

Lydia hadn't seen Alexander for two whole days. Two days where the only thing she could do was remember his kiss. She laid her fingertips over her lips as she sighed wistfully. She'd been so distracted by her thoughts that she'd given out the same assignment twice.

Daisy Drumm had been the one to point this out to her. "Miss Lydia, we already did our tens."

Glancing down at her papers, Lydia saw the child was right. "Thank you for bringing the mistake to my attention, Daisy."

"You're welcome, Miss Lydia."

"I'd like you all to start the next chapter in your reading lesson." This request brought about a myriad of moans from the students. She noticed Daisy and Laura seemed eager to please and were already turning to the pages where they'd last left off.

After a few more minutes the class settled down leaving her to more unsettling thoughts. Shaking herself out of the mood was harder than she'd thought it would be, and by the end of the day the children weren't the only ones anxious to be out of the classroom.

Waving good-bye to the last of the children, she gathered her schoolwork and locked the door. Instead of walking home as was her usual practice, she turned to the right, heading off in the direction of town.

It didn't take long to cover the distance to the sheriff's office. Even though Abigail was occupied with her new husband, she still managed to maintain regular hours at her job. Checking her time piece, Lydia saw that it was nearing four o'clock, almost time for Abby to be heading home. Hurrying her pace, she rushed onward hoping to catch her before she left.

Entering the building, Lydia was happy to see Maggie there, too.

"Good afternoon, Maggie, Abby," she said, taking off her bonnet and tossing it on the desktop.

"Lydia Louise, what brings you around for a visit?" Coming around from behind the desk, Abigail gave her a welcoming hug.

"Would you believe that I had some errands to run?"

"No," Maggie pertly replied.

"Guess you caught me in my little white lie." Taking the only other vacant seat, Lydia plunked herself down in the slat-backed chair across from Maggie.

Abigail returned to her perch behind the desk. "Man trouble."

"Why would you say something like that?" Maggie asked.

"Don't tell me you haven't seen that look before? You know the one where Lydia gets to frowning and sighing and nibbling on her lower lip."

Giving her a quick once over, Maggie nodded, smiling brightly. "Uh huh. Now I see what you mean!"

Disgusted with herself for being so transparent, Lydia complained, "Must you point out all my traits?"

"It's just that you're so adorable when faced with man trouble."

After wrinkling her nose at Abigail's comment, no matter how well-intentioned, Lydia let out a loud sigh.

"I'll have you know that not all men are like your husband—caring and easy to get along with. I bet you never have to guess what's on his mind."

"He does speak freely, that's for sure." Maggie agreed.

Abigail smiled. "And he is handsome and a very good kisser if I do say so myself!"

Lydia sighed yet again. Abigail was so head over heels in love with her husband that Lydia found herself feeling a twinge of envy.

Rolling her eyes, Maggie grinned. "That's more information than I needed to hear about your husband, Abby."

Abby snorted in a very unladylike manner.

"Someday, Miss Maggie you are going to fall head over heels in love, you mark my words."

Shaking her head fervently, she turned to Lydia. "Lydia's being here isn't about me. So spill it, dear cousin, what mess have you gone and gotten yourself into this time?"

Fussing with the seams on the side of her dress, she looked at her cousins through lowered eye lashes. "Alexander Judson is a fine man, don't you agree?"

"Oh my," Maggie whispered. "Abby was right."

"I knew this had to do with a man!" Abigail declared gleefully. "This is so wonderful!"

Trying to ignore the fact that both women were leaning forward in their seats, wanting to hear more, Lydia went on to explain how she'd been helping out at the Judson's home, ending with the part about the kiss. When she'd finished speaking the only sound greeting her was silence.

Lydia stood up and began pacing. "I know this is all so sudden and confusing, but truly I did nothing to provoke the man. One minute he was bandaging my finger and the next he was kissing me."

"She's falling . . ."

". . . in love," Maggie finished Abigail's statement.

Upon hearing the word "love" Lydia spun around facing them with both hands clenched on her hips. "I am not falling in . . ." flustered by the very thought of being in love, she found that even speaking the word was too much. Waving her hand wildly in the air, she finished with, "the word you said."

This comment set both women to smiling and nodding their heads.

"There is nothing to smile about!"

Abigail came around to place her arm around Lydia. "Of course there is. Don't you see, Lydia? You've always protected your heart and now when you've least expected it, love may have found you."

"This could be love. You have to admit that no other man has ever sent you running to us for advice."

The thought gave her pause. They were right. Lydia had never asked anyone for advice when it came to matters of the heart. She'd never needed any before. Whether or not she was falling for Alexander Judson remained to be seen. The only thing clear at this point was that she was definitely attracted to the man.

And the next thought to enter her mind was, what was she going to do about it?

Standing, Maggie started toward the door. "Come along, Lydia. Your dilemma isn't going to be solved today."

Looking to Abigail for help she was sadly disappointed when she only gave a quick shrug of her shoulders. "I'm afraid Maggie is right. Go home. If there's truly something between you and Alexander we'll all know soon enough."

Sighing, Lydia said, "Such sage advice."

"You asked for it, Lydia." Grabbing her by the arm Maggie pulled her out the door.

She may have asked for it, but was hoping their advice would have been a bit more fruitful. Walking down the street with Maggie they passed by the building that would soon house Surprise's newest business venture, the new dance hall.

Nudging Maggie's arm, she asked, "How are the plans coming along?"

Frowning, Maggie sniffed. "They are on hold for the moment. Aunt Margaret and I are having a disagreement over the design of the building."

Leave it to Aunt Margaret's namesake to go up against the matriarch of Surprise. "Is this stalemate going to end any time soon?"

"I don't think so."

They passed by the old saloon and were nearing the fork in the road, where Main Street branched off with High Road and the school to the right and Low Road and the boarding house to the left, when Lydia had the feeling they were being watched.

Without thinking, she turned her head to the right and looked across the street in the direction of Judson's Lumber Yard. Her stomach flip-flopped and her palms grew sweaty. Standing silhouetted in the doorway was the mill owner himself. Not knowing if she should acknowledge him with a wave or just keep walking left her feeling like an inexperienced schoolgirl.

Disgusted with herself, she picked up the pace, anxious to be safely inside Aunt Margaret's home. Once there, they left bonnets and paperwork on the table in the foyer. Knowing right where Aunt Margaret would be at this time of day, both women entered the cozy sitting room off of the backside of the foyer.

"Maggie, Lydia, good afternoon." Aunt Margaret was sitting near the fireplace in a chintz-covered settee. "I was wondering where the two of you were."

"We were visiting with Abigail," Maggie offered.

"And how is she?"

"Blissfully happy." Lydia sighed, plunking down at the opposite end of the settee. Eyeing the tray of tea cookies, she grabbed two and proceeded to polish them off without further ado.

Glancing from Maggie to Lydia, Aunt Margaret raised her eyebrows. "Trouble?"

Quick to ward off any concern her aunt might have regarding her love life, Lydia said, "None whatsoever."

"Good." Sitting up tall, Aunt Margaret continued, "I take it all is well at the school?"

"Yes." Lydia spent the next few minutes relating all of the antics and adventures of her students. "They're really very bright children."

"I'm so delighted to hear about their successes. As I'm sure their parents are too."

Uncertain of where her aunt was going with this thread of conversation, Lydia nodded her head in agreement.

"I imagine they'd like to see these accomplishments."

"I suppose so."

"Have you given any thought to doing an open house of sorts?"

"Actually I have been considering it." Even though the idea was proposed by her aunt, Lydia thought it had merits. What better way was there to show off the school than to invite the community in?

And so it was that the next few days was spent organizing the event taking her mind off of one Alexander Judson.

Chapter Ten

The children threw themselves into getting ready for the open house with so much enthusiasm that Lydia couldn't help getting caught up herself. Each child was responsible for the cleaning of his or her desk. The older children helped with washing the windows and sweeping the floor clean.

The day before the open house she was at the school putting the finishing touches on the decorations. Lydia had her hair tied back in an old handkerchief. She'd worn her oldest dress over which was tied a plan white apron that she'd borrowed from Anna.

Satisfied that each window had enough flower cutouts hanging from each pane, she stood back to admire their handiwork.

"This is beautiful."

"Yes, it is."

She spun around in surprise. "Mr. Judson. You frightened me. I didn't hear you come in." Her heart thumping, she quickly brushed some dust off of the apron.

He was looking at her and not the decorations. "I stopped by to let you know that The Mercantile will be sending over punch bowls and cups later today."

His deep brown eyes gazed over her. In them she thought she saw something—desire perhaps? A shiver of delight ran down her spine.

Finding her voice she answered, "Good. There will be a table for refreshments out in the backyard, the items can be left there."

Alexander continued to watch her and wondered if she was remembering the kiss they'd shared? He hadn't been able to think of much else for the past week, wavering between having enjoyed it and feeling guilty for betraying his wife's memory.

She was standing there smiling at him and he could sense the uncertainty in her. Alex didn't know what he was supposed to do next.

"Mr. Judson, is there something else I can do for you?"

Her voice startled him. "You can start calling me by my given name, Lydia." He hadn't realized until now just how much he'd missed hearing his name spoken by a female. Considering she'd been in his home and there was the matter of the kiss, he didn't see any harm in her calling him by his first name.

The look of surprise flitted across her face. He imagined there wasn't much that caught Miss Lydia off guard, but he just did and knowing that made him smile.

"Alexander, is there anything else I can do for you?"

She was flirting shamelessly. Grinning he kept his answer short. "Not at the moment, Miss Lydia."

"Be sure and let me know if there is . . . something I can do."

It was his turn to be flustered. She was incorrigible. Changing the subject matter to a safer one, he commented, "Robert and Laura have talked of nothing else except the open house. I've never seen them so excited."

"I know. I haven't been able to get the children to do any work all week long. It's a good thing they're all doing well with their studies or else I'd have the whole lot of them staying after to catch up."

"You are doing a fine job, Lydia."

"You sound surprised."

Resting his hip on one of the desks, he rubbed

his hand over his chin. "You weren't my first choice."

"I was the *only* choice, Alexander."

Tipping his head back, he laughed. It felt so good and carefree. It had been a long time since he'd laughed. Soon Lydia joined in. What a sight they must be making, two adults laughing at nothing in particular.

He found himself smiling at her. "Have dinner with me tonight." The invitation was unexpected and yet the moment the words left his mouth, he knew there wasn't anyone else he'd rather share a meal with.

Blinking she stared at him with her mouth open. Quickly closing it, she put her hand on her hips, tipping her head to one side, eyeing him suspiciously. "You're inviting me to dinner?"

"I guess I am."

"Why?"

Clamping his jaw shut, Alexander thought she would have been a bit more enthusiastic about the invitation. He wondered if she was even aware of what it had taken for him to suggest the dinner. *Why* indeed. What had he been thinking? Surely he and Miss Lydia were no match. She was flighty and spoiled by her aunt. He was raising two children and had the responsibility of running a business.

He very nearly had convinced himself to rescind

the offer when her voice penetrated his dark thoughts.

"What time should I be ready?"

"Seven o'clock."

He left the schoolhouse in a jumble of emotions and yet strangely elated. It had been a long time since he'd looked forward to anything. Every day since Joanna's death Alexander had been concentrating on putting one foot in front of the other, maybe it was time he move on with his life.

After getting Cole to agree to closing up for the day, he went home. Robert and Laura greeted him on the porch.

"Papa, you're home early!" Laura jumped into his arms before he'd even put one foot on the steps.

Had it really been such a long time since he'd surprised his children by coming home before dinner? If so then it was high time that changed for good. Delectable smells greeted him when he walked into his home.

Mrs. Sutherland was standing near the black cook stove. Steam rose in waves from the pot she was busy stirring. "Howdy, Mr. Judson."

"Afternoon, Mrs. Sutherland. I don't know what you're cooking up over there, but it smells mighty good." His mouth began to water.

"Just some stew and dumplings."

Alexander paused when he remembered the reason why he'd come home early. Then it hit him that he didn't have a clue how to make this evening's dinner for Lydia. He really hadn't thought much past asking her over. He began to worry that she was expecting him to take her to the one restaurant in town.

Mrs. Sutherland paused in her stirring and faced him with hands perched on well-rounded hips. "You're looking worried, Alexander."

Going to the stove he took the coffeepot off the back burner where it had been warming. Taking a thick white porcelain mug from the open shelf hanging above the stove, he proceeded to calmly pour himself a cup of the rich brew.

After taking a sip, he said nonchalantly, "I'm having company for dinner."

This bit of news caused the housekeeper to give a yelp. "Male or female?" Waving her hand in front of her face she added, "Oh never mind answering, I already know who it is."

Gulping, he looked at her wondering how she could possibly know he'd invited Lydia to dinner. He'd only asked her an hour ago. Surely news did not travel *that* fast in this town! Fear began niggling its way into his gut. He didn't want to have to explain his actions to anyone.

It was nobody's business but his own whom he invited into his home. He certainly didn't want to set any tongues wagging and surely he didn't want to have to face Miss Margaret. Setting the half drank cup of coffee in the sink he supposed it was too late to back out. Placing his hands on the edge of the sink he hung his head in despair.

"Mr. Judson, I didn't mean that everyone and their brother is aware of who you've asked to dinner. I guessed right away that it's Miss Lydia."

"How did you know?"

Going back to stirring the pot, old Mrs. Sutherland gave a quick shrug. "I figured with the open house scheduled for tomorrow you two have a lot of last minute details to iron out. That's all, Mr. Judson. Now you go spend some time with your youngsters while I finish supper."

"Lydia . . ." catching himself, he quickly corrected, "I mean Miss Monroe will be here around seven. I offered to pick her up."

"Tell you what, we'll get Robert and Laura fed and ready for bed, then you can have a quiet dinner with the teacher."

Realizing how lucky he was to have this woman, Alex walked over and gave her a big hug and kiss on the cheek. "Thank you. I don't know what we would do without you."

Blushing furiously, she pushed him away. "Now, now, Mr. Judson, there's no need for you to thank me. I'm just doing my job."

The next several hours flew by. By six-thirty Robert and Laura had been fed, washed and were obediently getting into their nightclothes. Mrs. Sutherland offered to stay until he arrived back with Lydia. He left the house just as she was preparing to re-set the table for two.

Blessedly, there was no one else around when he arrived at the big house on the hill. Looking at the massive structure, which was as far from his humble home as a building could get, set him to thinking Miss Margaret certainly didn't spare any expense in her home.

It had been a very long time since he'd been here. Adjusting his shirt sleeves, he stepped down from his wagon. The curtains at one of the second story windows fluttered closed. He was being watched. No doubt it was the matriarch herself checking his arrival.

The door opened before he was on the top step. Lydia stepped outside. "Before you tell me how it's proper for a lady to wait for the gentleman to call on her, let me say that I've just saved you from a fate worse than death."

"Let me guess, being interrogated by your Aunt Margaret and perhaps one of your cousins."

Laughing gaily, Lydia laid her hand in the crook of his arm as he led her down the steps and helped up on the wagon seat.

"You've no idea how persistent my family can be, Alexander. Oh they mean well," wrinkling her nose, she added, "but sometimes it's easier to avoid their good intentions altogether."

Never having experienced sibling or cousin rivalry, as was this case, Alexander really had nothing to compare it to. He envied Lydia her family and was glad that his children had each other to keep them company.

He listened intently when she began talking about the open house. The woman certainly threw herself into the project with unbound enthusiasm— so unlike Joanna who'd been reserved almost to the point of being shy.

"The children have done a wonderful job getting ready for the big day. They painted all the wall hangings and put out the best of their schoolwork for their parents to see."

Clapping her hands together she smiled. "We even have a few surprises."

"It sounds to me like you have everything under control."

"I hope so."

Pulling to a stop in front of his house, Alexander jumped down from the wagon, going around the other side to help Lydia to the ground. She laid her hands upon his shoulders, he didn't think twice about placing his hands along her waist and swinging her down.

They should have stepped away from each other, they didn't. Lydia's upturned face with those brilliant green eyes looked up at him expectantly. He could see the questions in her eyes. Was he going to kiss her? He wanted so desperately to do just that.

Lowering his head, he brought his mouth to hers. Before he had even tasted her sweetness, she gently pushed him away.

Gesturing towards the house, she whispered, "Alexander, we're being watched."

"What?" Reluctantly coming out of a fog of desire he looked down at her.

She pointed over his shoulder and he spun around to find Robert and Laura standing in the doorway.

Grinning, he apologized. "They were supposed to be in bed."

"I guess they wanted to see who you were bringing home for dinner."

Placing his hand on her back, he escorted Lydia into his home only to stop short in the doorway. Staring at the table he couldn't remember ever seeing it set in this manner. A white cloth had been placed on top of the pine surface and set upon that were two white plates, cloth napkins, silverware and two glasses. In the center sat a lantern, its wick set on a low flame.

Beside him, he heard the breath whoosh out of Lydia and wondered if she thought he was responsible for the table setting. Before either of them could say another word, Mrs. Sutherland appeared out of the back bedroom.

"I was just getting the children settled for bed."

Gathering them in her arms, she said, "Kiss your papa good-night." After doing as they were told, she whisked them down the hallway.

While he went over to the stove to turn the burner off, Lydia stood rooted to the spot just inside the entryway.

Gesturing towards the table, she said, "You didn't have to go to all this trouble for me."

Sheepishly he admitted. "We have Mrs. Sutherland to thank."

Placing her wrap on the hook behind the door, Lydia commented, "She outdid herself."

"The children are settled. Everything is ready to eat, whenever you are, Mr. Judson." Grabbing a small lantern off the wall, she lifted the globe, lighting the wick. "I'll just be going."

"Let me give you a ride home."

"That won't be necessary. Mr. Jules is going to escort me. He takes his evening walk every night at this time." Peering out into the dusky night, she said, "Here he comes now, right on time."

"Have a safe walk home."

"Good night. I'll see you in the morning." The door clicked shut behind her.

Lydia was standing behind one of the dining chairs, her hands resting lightly along the back.

The room suddenly felt too small for the two of them. Alexander leaned against the edge of the counter watching her, feeling like this were the first time he'd been alone with a pretty woman.

"Dinner smells delicious."

Springing into action he held out the chair for her and then brought the meal to the table. Half an hour later they were starting on the dessert, apple crisp.

"This is the first time I've invited a woman to my table since my wife died."

Setting her spoon alongside the dessert plate, Lydia looked across the short expanse of table. Her green-eyed gaze scanned his face. She didn't know how to respond to his confession. Folding her hands in her lap, Lydia was quiet.

"Her death must have been difficult for you."

Using the excuse to clear the table, Alexander's back was to her when he spoke again. "I think the children were the only reason I kept my sanity."

Pain at his loss knifed through her chest. Never having experienced a loss as great as his, she could only imagine what he'd been going through . . . how difficult it had been for him to go on. And for that reason, Lydia knew that she couldn't toy with his emotions.

This man wasn't about a mild, harmless flirtation. Fate had already broken his heart once. Getting up from the table, she picked up the empty glasses, carrying them to the sink. After putting them in the sink with the other dirty dishes, she stood beside him.

Laying a hand on his arm, she offered, "I'm terribly sorry about your wife."

He turned to face her, pulling her into his arms. Tentatively she returned the embrace, wrapping her arms about his waist, inhaling the all male scent of him. He laid a finger lightly under her chin, tipping her face so she was looking into his eyes.

She could see the questions there, and tried to imagine the self-doubt Alexander must be feeling right now. She thought how he must be questioning his motives for asking her here. Was he ready to move on with this part of his life? Could he be ready to fall in love, to give his heart freely and unburdened—to leave whatever lingering feelings he still harbored for his dead wife behind?

If Alexander wanted to begin a relationship with her, Lydia wanted him to come to her free of guilt. How could she tell him this without ruining their already tenuous relationship?

Chapter Eleven

The answer to her questions would have to wait.

In the next moment his mouth found hers. Leaning into the hard wall of his chest Lydia pressed against him. His mouth was hot and his kiss filled with such passion; she wanted to be the woman to release it. Kissing him, feeling the strength flowing from him, left her thinking this could be the man of her dreams.

Abruptly, he released her, resting his forehead on hers, they both fought to reign in their emotions.

"Alexander, what's happening between us?"

"I'm not sure," he whispered. "All I know is that, for better or worse, you drive me crazy."

"Let's hope it's crazy in a good way."

"Oh, yeah."

Toying with the stiff collar of his shirt, she sighed. She knew she should say something. Abruptly Alexander turned away, going to take her wrap from the hook. "It's getting late. I should take you home."

Already the warm feeling left by his body was cooling. Lydia didn't want to push him and yet she was left yearning for more. She sensed his heart was still fragile. She could only imagine the demons he was fighting.

Yes, she thought Alexander was right, it was time for her to go home.

All through the night she tossed and turned, Alexander's words playing over and over in her mind. His admission of his attraction to her was exactly what she'd been hoping to hear, but the part where he'd mentioned only feeling that way about one other woman—his wife, made her feel as if she'd something to prove.

She didn't know what his wife had been like. Obviously she'd been a caring, loving mother, that much was evident by watching Robert and Laura. The one thing Lydia did know is that she did not wish to take a dead woman's place, to be like her, that wouldn't be fair to any of them.

Quite certain that she was nothing like Alexander's wife, Lydia flung back the covers and got out of bed. If Alexander Judson was truly attracted to the person she was, then it was high time he got to meet the real Lydia Louise Monroe.

The first order of business was to put away the simple, conservative schoolmarm dress she'd pulled out of her wardrobe last night. Buttons up to the chin and long sleeves wouldn't be the order of the day. Today was a day calling for bright, vibrant colors, ones that would vie for attention with her red hair and compliment her green eyes.

Excitement surging through her veins, Lydia went to the spot where her favorite dresses hung in a neat row. She adored the blue one with the frilly white collar and cuffs, yearned to wear the satiny yellow dress, but it was the jade one that would adorn her today.

A beautiful creation, she'd had it made right before coming to Surprise. Ribbons of creamy white color formed a small checkered pattern throughout the skirt of the dress. It was a variation on the popular calico print, but so much more sophisticated.

The sleeves were three-quarter length, perfect for the spring weather. And the neckline was rounded, enticing enough to draw the eye of a gentleman, yet demure enough to be respectable. After donning stockings, undergarments, and a lightweight chemise, Lydia slipped into the day gown feeling quite the princess.

Turning in circles, she took a moment to savor the feeling of pure joy. Then it was time to put on her shoes and dress her hair. A simple chignon would suffice with the final touch of adding a simple decorative tortoise shell comb. A pinch of cheeks, a dot of color on her lips, and Lydia was ready to greet the new day!

"Maggie!" She called as she flew down the steps to the foyer. "I'm ready to go to the school if you're planning on coming with me we have to leave now."

"I'm coming. Land sakes, Lydia there's no need to be yelling." Maggie bustled out from the back parlor, patting her hair into place. "I've just left Aunt Margaret to finish with breakfast. Are you having any?"

Shaking her head, Lydia said, "I'm too nervous to eat. There will be plenty of food at the open house. I can get a bite later on."

"Wow." Maggie stopped walking and talking long enough to notice Lydia's appearance.

Frowning, Lydia paused in front of the hallway mirror for one last look. "Too much?"

"Perfect." Hugging her, Maggie sighed, "Just perfect."

Arm-in-arm they headed out the door to the schoolhouse. Hoping they'd be the first ones there, Lydia was surprised to find several buggies already tied up to the hitching post at the edge of the yard.

"I dare say people are excited, Lydia!"

Skipping on ahead of her cousin, Lydia fervently hoped Alexander was one of those people. The way they'd left things last night Lydia wasn't sure what he was thinking. Recognizing his wagon pulled near the front of the building, she paused a moment to collect herself. If she were to show him the real Lydia, she didn't want to scare him off.

A smile touched her lips when she saw him with Laura walking by his side. Her tiny hand was tucked up inside of his large one. Laura was telling her father something that made him smile. Turning her head, she spotted Lydia.

Releasing her father's hand, Laura ran to her. "Miss Lydia, I'm so excited about today, aren't you?" Wrapping her thin arms about Lydia's waist, Laura squeezed her.

Returning her hug, Lydia smoothed down the blonde locks of hair. "I am excited. We've a lot of people coming by to see the school today."

"Yes and my papa brought a whole bunch of stuff."

Lydia looked over the top of Laura's head to smile at Alexander. He was pushing the brim of his hat off his forehead, grinning. Surely this was a good sign.

Tugging at her hand, Laura bade her, "Come on, Miss Lydia. Wait till you see what we brought."

Following the child around to the front of the

building, Lydia stopped dead in her tracks. Her hand covering her heart she could hardly believe her eyes. Four water buckets filled with delicate white and blue wildflowers lined the steps leading to the front door.

"Oh my," she breathed out.

"Aren't they beautiful?" Laura looked from Lydia then back to the flowers.

Searching Alexander's face for any sign at all of what this meant for them, Lydia felt tears brimming her eyes. The simple gesture touched her so deeply that she couldn't seem to find any words to say.

Taking a step toward her, Alexander smiled. "I hope you don't think the flowers are too much decoration."

With a quick shake of her head Lydia regained her emotions. "They're perfect. Thank you."

"Papa and I picked them this morning," Laura advised her.

"I'm glad you did. The flowers add a welcoming feel to the front steps." Shielding her eyes against the mid-morning sun, Lydia squinted. "I can't believe there are so many people gathering already."

Taking her elbow, Alexander walked with her to the entrance. "It's a big day in Surprise." Stopping he turned to face her. Reaching out his hand, he brushed a stray lock of hair from her face. "And it's all thanks to you."

"The open house wasn't all my idea, Alexander."

Grinning he said, "Let me guess? Miss Margaret strikes again?"

"I'm afraid so." Instead of feeling angered by her aunt's loving interference, Lydia was surprised to find that she was feeling thankful for the suggestion. The open house was a good way for all the neighbors to get together and have some fun.

Leaning low, Alexander said softly, "In case I don't get a chance to say it; you look very pretty today."

Batting her lashes back at him, she beamed. "I'm glad you like my dress."

"I like more than just your dress, Lydia."

Longing to hear him say just what it was he liked about her, she was disappointed when they were interrupted.

Daisy Drumm's mother Eloise tapped her lightly on the arm garnering her attention. "Miss Lydia, I daresay you've done a fine job here. Why, I was just telling my husband, Jeffrey, what a nice teacher you are."

"That's very kind of you, Mrs. Drumm."

"No trouble at all." While Eloise tottered off in shoes too tight for her feet, Lydia turned, surprised to find a line of parents forming down the lawn.

An hour later with her cheeks sore from the constant smiling and her hand red from having it shaken by every adult in the town, Lydia made her way inside. There, parents milled about the wide classroom inspecting their children's schoolwork.

Maggie stopped by to tell her that the food was being set up on long tables out behind the building. Lydia couldn't help beaming with pride. Everything was going off without a hitch.

Quickly scanning the sea of faces she looked for Alexander, hoping to talk to him. When she didn't see him she made her way out to the backyard. Another minute of searching and she spotted him leaning against the trunk of a massive oak tree. Cole and Mr. Jules, who'd closed The Mercantile in honor of the event, were talking with him.

He looked so relaxed, carefree and handsome. Alexander Judson was one good looking gentleman. Her heart beat just a little faster remembering the kisses they'd shared. It was almost hard to believe this was the same man who'd greeted her so curtly when he found out she was the schoolteacher.

A blush stole across her face when he turned away from the other men and looked right at her. A smile played about his mouth. She imagined it was because he'd caught her staring at him. Whatever the cause, Lydia felt quite pleased knowing she was the woman who'd put it there.

Happiness burst to life inside of her. This was

the first time Lydia had ever felt this way about a man. Certainly this must be what love felt like.

"Miss Lydia, is it time yet?"

With a start she realized some of the children were surrounding her. Checking the watch she was wearing on a gold chain about her neck, Lydia saw the time had come to begin the entertainment.

The first order of business would be organizing a giant game of Duck, Duck, Goose. Giving the command for each child to bring his or her parents to the center of the yard, Lydia laughed at the antics some of them resorted to.

Eloise Drumm made it perfectly clear that she did not wish to be a part of such shenanigans, unfortunately for her, her husband ignoring the protests grabbed hold of her arm, dragging her to the circle.

Huffing and puffing the woman continued to carry on until finally Mrs. Sutherland told her to be quiet. "It's just a silly child's game, Eloise. I seriously doubt you'll come to any harm because of it."

Goodness, Lydia hoped no one would be injured playing the game. Clapping her hands together, Lydia called everyone to order. "Does everyone have a spot?"

The circle had widened to almost ungainly proportions, but that didn't seem to deter anyone from finding a place to stand. Eagerly the townsfolk awaited further instructions. After the rules were explained, everyone sat down on the ground.

Lydia was deciding who should run around tapping heads while chanting "duck, duck" and picking the "goose", first when little Lisa Albright shouted, "You should be the first one, Miss Lydia!"

Placing her hands on her hips, she laughed. "No. I'm the teacher."

"I think you should be first." Surprised when she recognized Alexander's voice, Lydia complied.

Walking slowly around the circle she started the chant. "Duck. Duck. Duck." Whacking Maggie on the head, she giggled. "Duck." Two more "ducks" followed and then shouting, "Goose!" she ran like her feet were on fire.

Before she could find a place to sneak into and sit, Alexander was upon her, grabbing her about the waist and lifting her off the ground.

"Put me down!"

Laughter and cheers rent the air. Her students were going wild at the sight of their teacher acting like one of them. Slowly the world righted itself. Alexander held her lightly in the safety of his arms.

"I think you're supposed to be playing the game," she sighed.

"I am." Winking at her, Alexander released his hold on her and took his turn.

After half an hour of playing, the parents wandered off to the tables sagging under the weight of casserole dishes. Standing behind the first table, Lydia handed out cups of punch.

"Well, I'd say that you and Alexander are getting along." Joining her at the table, Abigail started cutting pieces of watermelon.

"Yes, we are."

Maggie wandered over and put the thick slices of juicy red fruit on platters. "My, my, it looks to me like Mr. Judson is smitten with you."

"Seems to me that the schoolteacher should be paying attention to her children, not their parents."

Chapter Twelve

Her mouth hung open in shock as Lydia felt her face grow hot with embarrassment. Abigail came to her defense. "Lydia is a wonderful teacher."

Fluffing herself up like a peacock, the woman sputtered, "I'm just saying she needs to put the children's wants first."

Springing into action, Maggie wagged a finger in front of the woman's face. "You're just mad because you were forced to play along with the game."

"I am not."

Fearing that this would turn into a brawl, and wanting to avoid any bad behavior that could ruin the day, Lydia quickly interjected, "Maggie, Abigail please be quiet. Mrs. Drumm has every right to her opinion."

"Thank you."

Gently setting the ladle inside the punch bowl, Lydia pasted her brightest smile on her face. Sweet as Aunt Margaret's sugar-laced tea, she said, "However, Eloise. I can call you by your given name, can't I?"

Narrowing her eyes in suspicion the woman nodded.

"Eloise, while you are entitled to your opinion, I would appreciate it if you would consult with me in private the next time you feel the need to criticize."

"I wasn't criticizing."

Holding her hand up to silence the woman, Lydia spoke. "You are correct, of course. You were just expressing your opinion." If she smiled any harder, Lydia thought her face just might break. "Why don't you come by after school on Monday and we can continue this conversation."

Backing away from the table, Eloise shook her head. "That won't be necessary, Miss Lydia."

"Wow!" Maggie placed an arm protectively about Lydia's shoulders. "You sure put her in her place."

With long easy strides, Alexander made his way to the table where the Monroe cousins were huddled together talking softly, having what looked to be a serious conversation. One look at Lydia's face and he knew something was wrong.

"Maggie, Abigail." Tipping his hat to the women protectively flanking Lydia, he looked from one to the other, sure that something was wrong.

"If you don't mind I'd like a word with Lydia." Without waiting for an answer, he took hold of her arm, leading her away from the picnic area.

"Alexander, really there's no need to be manhandling me," she protested. Anxiously, she glanced over her shoulder.

He wondered who she was looking for in the crowd. "What's wrong?"

Pulling away from him, she kept her back turned. "Nothing is wrong. My cousins and I were just discussing how we thought the day was going."

Hands on hips he walked around so he could look her square in the eye. "Was Mrs. Drumm involved in your conversation?"

"No."

At the mention of the woman's name, he saw Lydia blanch. "I see. Did she say something to offend you?"

"Alexander, I really don't want to discuss this with you. Let's go back and have some food. Anna sent down some of her scrumptious sugar cookies."

He looked at her closely and saw the stubbornness in the set of her jaw. She wasn't going to tell him what transpired. So be it. He'd find out on his own.

"Cookies sound great." When he went to take her arm, she moved slightly out of his reach.

One thing was certain, whatever that old biddy Mrs. Drumm said to Lydia upset her. Not wanting it to ruin what was left of the day, Alex cajoled, "You sure play a mean game of duck, duck, goose."

Tilting her head up at him he caught the glint of mischievous in her green eyes. "It's a fun game. You're not so bad at it yourself."

"I haven't had as much practice as you have I'm afraid."

"You should take more time for play, Alexander, it will keep you young."

Harrumphing, he matched his stride to hers. "I play plenty."

Laughing at him, she responded, "You do not."

Not willing to let her have the last word on the subject, he countered. "I do, too."

"Now you sound like one of the children, arguing with me."

He let her walk ahead of him. Slowing his pace,

Alex admired the curve of the backside she presented. The jade striped fabric fluttered with the gentle sway of her hips. She was speaking to him and he didn't hear a word.

"Alexander, I asked you a question."

Stopping he stared at her, concentrating on her lips. "I'm sorry I didn't hear you." Fighting the urge to take her in his arms and kiss her right there in front of the entire town, he ran a hand over his mouth.

"I asked, when was the last time you went on a picnic?"

"Well, I'm attending one today, I don't suppose that counts?"

A firm shake of her head gave him the answer.

"I mean the last time you've taken a day off from work was . . . ?"

Anger prickled along the back of his neck. Why must she always be reminding him of the long hours he kept? "Come on now, Lydia, you know I can't very well take a day off for no good reason."

"Spending time with Robert and Laura would give you a good reason. You should pack a lunch, walk down to the pond and sit under the big ole shade tree growing there."

Leaving him to mull over the absurd suggestion, he watched as she walked off to join Mrs. White and Mrs. Sutherland. It didn't escape his notice that she cut a wide swath around Eloise Drumm.

By the following Wednesday, Alexander had had his fill of sawdust and the constant buzzing of the saws. The good news was they had more work than both of them could handle and the bad news was they had more work than both of them could handle. After a meeting yesterday with Cole, both men had decided they needed to hire more workers.

Realizing the current workload was fast becoming a permanent part of his life did little to improve Alex's bad mood. Ever since Lydia had challenged him to take a day off, it seemed like everyone in the town needed to have one thing or another built.

As far as he was concerned, the first order of business would be posting help wanted signs around town. Making some up, Alex took them around to the boarding house, the sheriff's office and lastly The Mercantile.

After leaving the store, he found his thoughts returning to his workload. He tipped his hat to Mr. White as he walked into the store with his oldest daughter. Alex couldn't help but envy the man his spare time. It would be nice to take Laura shopping even if it were for nothing more than to pick out a stick of candy.

As for his son, Robert had come to the age

where he needed his father's influence more and more with each passing day. Sighing, he couldn't believe how fast time seemed to be speeding by. Lydia was right; he needed to take some time for his family, even if it were just a few hours for a picnic.

Back at his office he found Cole loading the last of the boarding house order into the wagon. "I'm glad to see this order is going out."

Removing his hat, Cole wiped his arm across his brow. "I am, too. I hope she's happy with the wood. I know it's going to be used in one of her new guest rooms."

"At least it's one more order we can cross off our list."

Nodding in agreement, Cole asked, "Did you get the posters up?"

"I did. Let's hope by the end of the week we'll have had some inquiries. The way I figure, if we can hire two employees that will be a big help."

Flipping a thick length of rope over the top of the load, Alexander caught the end and tied it off. Giving it a quick tug, he made sure the load was secure. "I've got to run up to my house to check on something. Can you handle this while I'm gone?"

"No problem. Everything all right?"

"Yup." Without offering any further explanation, Alex headed off to his house.

When he arrived he found Mrs. Sutherland in his kitchen preparing supper.

Hearing him enter, she turned in surprise. "Mr. Judson, I didn't expect you home this early."

Feeling a little embarrassed, he laid his hat on the table. "I need a favor."

Wiping her hands on a towel, she poured him a cup of coffee. "Anything at all, Mr. Judson, ask away."

"I was thinking of surprising Robert and Laura by taking them on a picnic. I see you've already started supper, would it be too much trouble to make it a picnic supper instead?"

He had to hand it to the woman who didn't so much as bat an eye at his out of the blue request.

"Fried chicken is perfect picnic food and that's all I was cooking up for dinner." Rummaging around in the cabinet under the sink, she added, "I thought I saw a wicker hamper in here a while back. Yup, here it is."

Pulling the basket from its resting place, she turned to him smiling triumphantly. "Just needs to be dusted off a bit and then it'll be ready to pack up."

Seeing the gem he had in her, Alexander walked over and gave her a quick kiss on the cheek. "Thank you. I plan on leaving work early. So I'll be home by four o'clock sharp."

"The children are going to be so happy that

you're taking them on a picnic." Cocking her head to one side she looked at him curiously. "Might I ask what or dare I say, who prompted this happy event?"

Giving her a quick wink, he replied, "A certain red-haired school teacher," which reminded him the picnic wouldn't be the same without the woman who'd given him the idea there to enjoy it with them.

There was no one inside or outside the classroom when he arrived. So he wrote a quick note inviting her to join them for supper, folded the paper, wrote Lydia's name on the outside, and left it propped against an open book on her desk where she'd be sure to find it.

As he headed down the front steps, he heard the joyous sounds of the children. Turning his head to the right, he could just make out the tops of their heads. Of course it was hard to miss Lydia's. The dappled sunlight turned her hair to shades of warm, coppery red.

Not wanting to disturb their lesson, he hurried back to his office hoping that she would accept his offer. If he were taking his family on a jaunt to the pond, Lydia Louise Monroe was the only woman he wanted to share the time with; over the past months it had become clear to him that his children were growing very fond of her.

Their relationship was more than that of a

teacher and her students. When Lydia was with them, he could see from the joy on her face that she was truly happy. More importantly, the same look was reflected clearly in Robert's and Laura's faces, too.

A long time had passed since they'd had sunshine in their lives. Lydia brought out the best in them. While humming a little ditty, Alexander realized he felt something he hadn't thought he would ever feel again—love and happiness. He owed it all to Lydia Louise Monroe.

Chapter Thirteen

Thrilled to see that Alex had taken her suggestion to go on a picnic, Lydia was still surprised when she read his note for the third time. He was inviting her along. She could only hope that this meant what she thought it did—he was beginning to trust her and his feelings.

This could be the start of something wonderful. Excited beyond belief, she could hardly wait to dismiss the class for the day. She gathered her papers and went to find Laura and Robert.

When she walked them home, she told them about their papa's surprise.

"A picnic?" As she jumped up and down, it was clear that Laura was as excited as Lydia.

"Yes. A picnic down by the pond."

"I'm going to change into play clothes. There's a big bullfrog I've been hearing every night for the past week, and I want to catch him." Robert ran ahead of the ladies and reached the house well before they did.

It could have been her imagination, but Lydia felt certain that the sky looked a little bluer and the birds were chirping a bit more merrily than they'd been an hour earlier. She felt ready to burst with all of the happiness welling up inside of her.

Taking Laura's hands in hers, she spun her around and around. "We're going on a picnic!"

Peals of delight came from the little girl. "Papa is taking time from his work, Miss Lydia."

"I know. Isn't it wonderful?"

"Yippee!" Letting go of her, Laura ran into the house after her brother to change into play clothes as well.

By the time she caught up to them, they were ready to go. Mrs. Sutherland greeted her at the door.

"Good afternoon, Miss," Mrs. Sutherland greeted her.

"Hello, Mrs. Sutherland."

"Mr. Judson wants you to meet him down by the pond. I've packed up supper and found a quilt that you can spread on the ground."

"How kind of you." The aromas floating out of the basket made her mouth water. The children pushed past them and ran outside. Laughing at their antics, Lydia said, "I think those two are more than ready to go."

Placing her hands on rounded hips, Mrs. Sutherland agreed. "This is good for them. You're good for them . . . and for Mr. Judson."

Surprised by her comment, Lydia found herself momentarily speechless.

Joining her on the porch, the kindly woman looked at her with concern. "I didn't mean to embarrass you."

"You didn't," she lied.

"It's just that I haven't seen this family so happy in a very long time. I think you're responsible for that."

"Mrs. Sutherland, you flatter me. But I think they are just finally allowing themselves to heal. I imagine they all had a horrible time after Alexander's wife died."

"Yes, they did. Until you came to town, I thought he was going to let the grief swallow him whole." Fussing with her apron, she added, "I'm glad you're a part of their lives."

Stunned into silence, Lydia accepted the basket and blanket from her and turned to follow the children down to the pond. Finding them standing near the edge of the water, Lydia hurried over to them.

"Don't step too close to the water." She set the

basket on the grassy knoll and peered over their shoulders to see what they were looking at.

"I told you it would be a big one!" Robert had a stick in his hand. Using it to push the bright green algae away from the edge of the pond, he exposed a large, dimply pond scum-covered green frog.

His sister shrieked at the sight of it, and jumped back from the edge of the pond. "I hate frogs! Yuck. You can have it, Robert."

Lydia laughed and offered, "Why don't you help me set up our picnic?"

The idea must have appealed to Laura, for she skipped happily ahead of Lydia with the blanket in hand. Finding a smooth patch of ground, Laura started to spread the blanket.

"Here, let me help you." Setting the basket against the trunk of the tree, Lydia took one end and fluffing it into the air, waited for the soft cotton fabric to settle on the tender blades of grass.

Walking around all four edges, she smoothed it out as best she could. "There, that should do."

"I can climb trees." Laura declared while swinging from a low branch. Her small hands gripped the bark with all her might while she swung back and forth like a monkey. "Robert's been showing me how."

Peering up through the leafy branches, Lydia remembered all the summers she'd spent climbing trees with Maggie and Abigail. *My, but that was a long time ago*, she thought, envying Laura's energy.

Today, climbing trees was the last thing on her mind. Right now, she was wondering about Alexander, dreaming about how he felt about her, if he were ready to let her into his life. Thinking he might just, if luck were on her side, want her to be his next wife and a mother to his children.

While the wonderful, dreamy thoughts swam around in her head, Lydia hugged her arms about her waist losing herself to the giddy feeling of being in love. She didn't notice Laura when she let go of the low branch, or when she'd moved around to the far side of the tree out of sight.

It wasn't until a shout from somewhere above her head reached her that she became aware that Laura wasn't where she'd last seen her. Looking up into the maze of branches, Lydia's heart caught in the throat.

"Laura Judson what are you doing way up there?"

The child had to be eight feet off the ground. While the height might not seem high to Laura, it was terrifying for Lydia to see her up there.

"I told you I knew how to climb trees. Look at me, Miss Lydia! I'm like a bird." Laura began to flap her arms like a bird. "Chirp, chirp," she sang out.

Lydia felt the panic grip her. Dear God! What if she fell? Taking a deep breath, she released it and called out, "Laura, honey, you need to come down from there right now."

Oblivious to her request, Laura sang louder and flapped her arms faster, harder. A loud crack followed by a snapping noise rended the air.

"Laura!" Lydia shrieked, running to where the little girl was falling out of the tree. Oh no! She wasn't going to reach her in time. Lurching forward, with her arms flung out, Lydia made every effort to catch her.

The muscles in her upper arms and shoulders were straining, flexing, stretching as far as was humanly possible. She thought everything would be all right. Just then, a worn piece of fabric and petticoats slipped through her fingers.

Alexander was coming up the hill by the pond. Spotting Robert, he gave a quick "hello" and waved to his son, who appeared to be having himself a grand time tormenting a bull frog. Pulling his hat from his head, he ran a hand through his hair searching for Lydia and Laura.

Passing by Robert he shouted, "Where are your sister and Miss Lydia?" He'd gotten stuck at work and had to rush a customer out the door so he could get here for the picnic.

Alex had looked forward to nothing else all afternoon.

"Up under the tree, Laura's acting like a girl. She's afraid of my frog."

Alex laughed. Of course Laura was acting that way she was a little girl—his little girl, growing up so fast with her mother's eyes and his smile. He caught a flash of red hair and knew he'd found them.

He saw Lydia kneeling on the ground and wondered what she was doing. Thinking she might need some help unpacking their supper, he hurried along. By the time he reached her, he realized she wasn't unpacking the basket at all.

"Lydia! What's going on?" He'd felt as if he'd been punched in the stomach, the breath whooshed from his lungs.

Sobbing, Lydia answered, "She fell from the tree."

"Dear God!" Pushing her aside, Alex knelt beside his daughter who was crying softly. Without another thought, he scooped her up into his arms.

Pushing Lydia aside, he started running towards his house. Sweat poured from him as his feet pounded along the ground. *This couldn't be happening again,* was all he kept thinking.

"Laura, Papa is here. You're going to be all right." Crooning those words to her, Alex kept moving at the frantic pace until he reached the porch. He ran up the steps two at a time and shoved the door open with his shoulder, bounding into the house.

Settling in the chair by the fireplace, he took a closer look at his daughter. Her breath was coming in big gulps. "Laura, tell me where you're hurt."

Her face was splotchy from crying. In quick, jerky motions she pointed to her right arm. Alex sucked in his breath when he saw the twist in her arm.

Vaguely aware of Lydia and Robert hovering behind them, he barked, "Robert, run to town and get the doctor."

The boy was out the door before Alex had finished getting the command out. Gently, he started rocking his wounded daughter. Pulling her close to his chest, the sounds of her crying muffled against him. He felt his heart breaking all over again.

How could this be happening to them? The only thing he could see was Laura lying on the ground like a rag doll. Where had Lydia been? How could she have allowed this to happen?

He saw the hand reaching out to smooth Laura's hair from her brow. Reaching out, he caught her wrist in his hand. "I can take care of my daughter." Just like he was supposed to have taken care of his wife?

He'd been late when Joanna had fallen and died.

And he'd been late today. It was almost unthinkable that the same tragedy could have befallen him yet again. The pain and shame of his guilt took away any sane thoughts.

Beneath his grip her cold hand trembled.

Repeating the words, as if to remind himself of his responsibilities, he whispered, "I can take care of her." Pushing aside the hand that reached out to help him, he begged Lydia, "Please leave us alone."

Looking up into those familiar green eyes he willed himself not to care that they were brimming with tears and that her face was pale with fear, he ordered in a broken voice, "Leave."

"Alexander, you don't mean that." Her voice was a whisper, the tears spilling unchecked down her cheeks.

Ignoring her, he buried his face in his daughter's hair choking back a strangled sob unable to speak.

Backing away from them, Lydia went to stand silhouetted in the open doorway, watching for Robert and the doctor. As she hugged herself about the waist, Robert looked up to see her quietly sobbing.

It almost killed him to be so mean to her. But Alex couldn't bring himself to allow her to comfort him. He didn't deserve her sympathy. This was his fault. Laura yelped in pain. Readjusting them in the chair, he found a position that seemed to be better for her.

"Here comes the doctor." Stepping aside, Lydia made room for the doctor and Robert to enter. "She's over there." Pointing with an unsteady hand, Lydia showed the doctor to Laura and Alex.

Doc Adams, an older gentleman who'd delivered most of the children in the town, spoke in a deep soothing voice, "Let's move her into one of the bedrooms."

Doing as he was told, Alexander went through the first doorway off the hall. He gently laid his daughter's broken body down on the bed her parents once shared.

"Papa, don't leave me," she wailed.

Keeping her good hand tucked safely inside his, Alex sat on the edge of the bed. "I'm right here. Papa's not going anywhere. I'm going to stay by your side as long as you need me."

"I want my mama." Her plaintive cry shattered his heart, gripping his soul in so much sorrow that he felt the pain sear through him as if it were cutting him in half.

Focusing all of his strength on Laura, he struggled to find the right words. "I'm here. Papa's here."

Hastily the doctor cut away the sleeve of her dress exposing the broken arm. Sucking in his breath at the sight of it, Alex wanted to be sick.

How could a bone twist in such a manner? Oh, the pain his brave little girl must be enduring. Once again he was awash with the need to make that pain his.

"Alexander, I need to set this arm," the doctor said as he pushed the wire rimmed glasses up the bridge of his nose, and laid a gentle hand on Alex's shoulder.

"Is it going to be painful for her?" Alex knew the question was ridiculous, and still he couldn't help asking it.

After rolling up his shirt sleeves about his elbows, the doctor opened his black bag. He pulled out a brown bottle and tipped some of the liquid onto a piece of white cloth. "I'll sedate her first. I can try to make this as painless as possible, but I'm not going to sugar-coat this, she is going to feel what I'm about to do."

Sickened by the thought, Alex gulped in deep breaths. "All right." Reaching out, he brushed some locks of blonde hair off Laura's dampened brow. "The doctor's going to get you all fixed up."

Placing the white cloth over her mouth and nose he ordered her to breathe deeply. Doing as she was told, within a few minutes her eyes drifted shut. Alex watched as she relaxed her grip on his hand.

With a quick nod of his head, the doctor set her arm. Laura gave a sharp yelp when the bone snapped in place. Alexander felt as if the room were spinning, the doctor's face blurred before his eyes. A strange buzzing sound came to him.

He forced himself to take deep, even breaths until the sensation passed. He watched forlornly while the doctor splinted the arm and made a sling for it.

When that was finished, he turned to Alex, saying, "She'll be more comfortable if we can get her out of the dress and into her nightgown. The medicine I gave her will wear off in about an hour, and then you can give her the painkiller I'll leave here."

Barely able to absorb what the man was saying, Alexander nodded. Then, rising from the bed he helped get Laura changed. Tucking the blankets around her still form, he placed a pillow under her arm as instructed.

"It's important to keep the arm elevated for the next week or so. No activity whatsoever. Visitors will do her some good after a day or two. Right now she needs bed rest and to remain quiet." Leaving a paper with instructions on the nightstand, the doctor snapped his bag shut.

Pausing in the doorway he said to Alex, "I'll be back in the morning to check on her. If you need anything at all send Robert or Miss Lydia to fetch me."

Focusing on his daughter, he wasn't even aware when the man left the house. Leaving her bedside,

Alex pulled a wicker rocking chair beside the bed. Sitting down, he caught sight of the picture of Joanna. Reaching for the silver frame, he hugged it to his chest.

How could he have thought he was ready to fall in love again? If he hadn't been late yet again none of this would have happened. He didn't deserve to be loved by any woman.

Chapter Fourteen

Gently he rocked back and forth, while life went on around them. From the kitchen came the sounds of dishes being washed and put away. He heard Robert talking to someone, probably Mrs. Sutherland. Crickets and tree frogs chirped and croaked, making familiar nighttime noises.

Sometime in the last few hours, darkness had fallen and Alex hadn't even noticed. Rising, he took the globe off the lantern on the nightstand. He was going to light the wick, but couldn't find a match and flint.

Making sure that Laura was comfortable first, he left the room going to the kitchen and stopped dead in his tracks when he saw Lydia sitting at the table with Robert. He had thought she had left.

Instead, he found himself looking at what could have been any other normal nighttime ritual.

Robert had his head bent over some papers while Lydia sipped tea from a cup. The only problem was, this wasn't another normal night in the Judson household.

"Robert, you should be in bed."

Surprised by the sound of his father's voice, Robert raised his head. "I was just working on some schoolwork with Miss Lydia."

"It's late. Go to bed," Alex ordered.

"Yes, sir." He pushed the papers into a pile and did as he was told.

Rising from her seat, Lydia went to the stove and poured a cup of coffee. Turning she held the thick white mug out to him.

He took the cup because she offered it. Going through the motions, he sipped the strong brew. Frustration at not being able to help his daughter broiled inside of him.

Laying a hand on his sleeve, she spoke. "There's no need to be so hard on him, Alexander. He's worried about his sister."

"I know that." Turning on her, he pulled free from her grasp. "I thought you'd gone home." He spoke in a halting voice.

She looked stunned by his comment. Seeing the hurt look in her eyes, Alexander forced himself not to care.

"I was about to help Robert get ready for bed."

"It's been a long day for all of us. Go home, Lydia."

"If this is really what you want me to do, then I'll leave."

"It is."

She stared to reach out to him and he backed away, imploring her, "Lydia, please, I'm begging you, go now." The uncertainty lingered in the expression on her face. He almost gave into the temptation to take her in his arms, to hold her close, taking whatever comfort he could find.

He couldn't do any of those things because he couldn't bear to let her see his shame.

Still standing before him, she tried to explain what had happened to Laura. "I'm sorry, Alex. I should have been taking better care of her, but I swear to you what happened was an accident."

He could have argued the point with her, telling her that children sometimes moved quicker than lightening, that it was hard to keep track of them all the time. But he took the coward's way out; it was easier than admitting his own guilt to her.

"You're right. You should have been paying closer attention to her."

"Alex." She spoke his name on a whisper. "Please, let me stay and make this right."

Shaking his head, he walked to the door and

opened it waiting for her to leave. Clenching his hands by his side, he watched her walk away, delivering the final blow sure to keep her away from him. "I want you to find another job."

Her steps faltered when she heard him, but Lydia didn't stop, or turn around to confront him. She just kept walking away.

What had started out as a day of hope and anticipation had turned into the worst day of her life. And now that she no longer needed to put up a brave front, Lydia gave into the tears she'd been fighting to hold back.

Sobbing, she ran from his house and didn't stop running until she was inside of Aunt Margaret's home. Covering her hand over her mouth to stifle the sobs she stood in the great hallway crying her heart out.

"Oh my gosh, Lydia! Lydia what's happened?" Maggie hurried down the stairs and quickly taking things from her, led her into the back parlor. "Hush, now. Nothing can be this bad."

Gulping in breaths of air, Lydia couldn't calm herself. Hysterical, she flung herself face down on the chintz-covered sofa. Her wails echoed off the walls and brought Aunt Margaret and Anna scurrying into the room to see what the commotion was about.

"Maggie, what's wrong?" Pushing up from the wheelchair Margaret came to Lydia's side.

"I don't know. She can't seem to stop crying." Wringing her hands together in a manner that was so unlike her, Maggie said, "Aunt Margaret, do something!"

Speaking sternly, she said, "Lydia, stop this crying at once. You're scaring us."

It seemed as if an eternity had passed since she'd left Alexander's when in reality it was only half an hour. Half an hour of feeling like her world had been torn out from under her, half an hour of nonstop crying.

Half an hour of living with a broken heart.

Lydia didn't think she could find the words to tell them what had happened. In the time since she'd come home, Anna had brewed up a strong pot of black tea which Aunt Margaret had insisted be liberally laced with brandy and Abigail had been summoned.

"I didn't know if we would be needing the law or another woman." Aunt Margaret's brow puckered into a frown when Abigail arrived.

Slowly, Lydia pushed herself into a sitting position, gratefully accepting the cool cloth Maggie was handing to her. Accepting the pats of sympathy and taking a generous sip of the brandy laced tea, Lydia managed a deep, albeit, shaky breath.

Looking around at the caring faces surrounding her, Lydia feared she would start crying all over again. It was Maggie who held up her hand stopping her.

"Please, don't start crying. I couldn't bear to see you in such a state again."

On a good day Lydia would have balked at her insensitivity, but right now she figured it was well deserved. Crying wasn't going to solve this problem anyway. A shudder went through her as the full implication of what had just happened hit her.

"It was my entire fault," she hiccupped.

Sitting next to her on the sofa, Abigail asked, concern etching lines in her forehead, "What happened?"

Wringing her hands together, she began to explain. "We were waiting for Alexander down by the pond. He'd invited me to a picnic with him and his children."

"My, my, are you telling me that the man was actually going to do something fun?"

Lydia bobbed her head up and down in answer to her aunt's question. "I know. I was so glad to see he was finally coming around." Fresh tears spilled over her eyes as she thought about how quickly the day had soured. "And then something . . ." her lip quivered . . . "horrible happened."

"What! What happened, Lydia?" Maggie prompted impatiently.

Covering her mouth with her hand, she whispered, "Laura fell from the tree."

Gasps and sympathetic coos erupted from the three women. "Why is this your fault?" Aunt Margaret wanted to know.

"I was supposed to be watching her. Alex was meeting us there, he was running late and Robert was playing with a frog he'd caught. Laura was with me by the tree." Feeling sick to her stomach, Lydia reached for her teacup.

Taking another sip she waited a few moments before saying, "I'd only turned away for just a second and then she was up the tree yelling down at me. Showing me how she could act like a bird. I told her to come down. And then . . ."

Unable to continue, she was relieved when Abigail finished her sentence. "And then she fell. Lydia, it was an accident, surely Alexander knows this?"

Shaking her head with enough force to loosen her hair from its bun, Lydia said, "I'm not sure what he's thinking right now. He has every right to be upset. I know how terrible I felt watching that little girl laying in her father's arms in pain."

"Yes, well I'm certain Alexander is feeling a

sense of history repeating itself." Aunt Margaret sighed.

Shaking her head, Lydia said, "I don't understand. We were finally coming to terms with our feelings towards one another. And then this happened and Alex turned me away."

"Wait, tell us how Laura is doing." Sensible Maggie wanted to know.

"Her arm is broken."

This elicited a more gasps and "oh mys" from the women. "The poor child," Aunt Margaret concurred.

"I know this is horrible. The doctor came and set her arm while I waited with Robert. Then Alexander came out and said I should leave."

"Well this is his child who was hurt. You can't blame the man for being upset."

"Abby, that I can understand. It was more than his being upset that one of his children was in pain. I can't explain it." Thinking back to how quickly he'd withdrawn reminding her of the man she'd first met all those weeks ago.

Quietly, Aunt Margaret said, "I think I know why he acted the way he did. Trust me when I say this has nothing to do with you, Lydia. You had no way of knowing about the circumstances of his wife's death."

The death of his wife was something they'd never discussed. She knew only that when she'd arrived in Surprise he'd been a cold, unhappy man barely able to smile.

"Tell me what happened to her, Aunt Margaret."

As moonlight spilled into the room and with the lanterns spreading their warming glow, Margaret told her nieces the story of Alexander and Joanna Judson.

By the time she reached the part where the poor woman died, there wasn't a dry eye between them. "You see, Lydia, Joanna was out at the pond with her children the day she died."

"Laura was just a bit of a girl, toddling around at her mother's feet while Robert napped at her side. What possessed her to go up into the tree no one will ever know, but she was climbing down when she fell and hit her head."

Lydia gasped at the horrible image her aunt presented to them of a young mother dying in front of her children.

"And Alexander found her dead."

Lydia's gut ached over the pain he suffered. But knowing that she was the cause of his pain now was her undoing. Sobs wracked her body. This time she gratefully accepted the comforting hugs from her cousins.

The pain ripped through her heart, searing her soul. All she could think about was Alexander and how much she'd come to care for him. How he'd learned to trust again and what her one ridiculous mistake had cost them. She should never have taken her eyes off of Laura, not for one second.

This was her fault, and somehow Lydia had to find a way to make it right.

Chapter Fifteen

"**P**apa, where's Miss Lydia?" Propped against a mountain of pillows, with her golden curls spread about her face like an angel, Laura batted her blue eyes up at him.

Carefully smoothing the blankets under her chin, Alex forced a smile. "She's busy, sweetie."

Five days had passed since Laura broke her arm and Lydia had stayed away. Her absence was what he'd wanted, wasn't it? What he hadn't realized was how fond Robert and Laura had grown of the woman. Laura had asked for Lydia several times each day and Robert moped around the house. He was running out of excuses for her absence.

Since Robert had seen fit to inform his sister of the fact that they'd had a substitute teacher since the beginning of the week, Laura was smart enough to know that Lydia wasn't busy at school. Alex imagined in a child's mind it meant Miss Lydia must have a lot of free time and she should be here visiting with Laura.

Well that wasn't the case. Alex had no way of knowing how Lydia was passing her time these days because he hadn't seen her. And that was just fine by him. Over the past few lonely days he'd managed to convince himself that Lydia Louise Monroe was trouble; he'd known it from the minute she breezed into town.

"I want to see her, Papa. Can't you see if she can come today?" Big, baby blue eyes looked up at him. He thought his heart just might break.

Doing something he'd never in his life done, Alex lied to his daughter. "She's helping her cousin, Maggie with the new dance hall. I think she's pretty busy."

"Too busy to see me?" Tears welled in her eyes.

Running his hand over his face, Alex realized he shouldn't make Laura suffer because he was angry. "I'll see what I can do."

"Thank you, Papa. When you see her can you ask her to bring me a peppermint stick?" Smiling as only a little girl did when she wanted something, she said, "I finished the one you brought me yesterday."

Chuckling at her antics, he responded, "I'll see

what can be done about that. You know if you eat too many of those peppermint sticks your teeth are going to fall out of your head?"

Giggles erupted from her. "Oh, Papa my teeth aren't going to fall out."

"All right, we'll have to wait and see." Rising from her bedside, he checked to make sure she had water in the glass on the stand. Then kissing her on the forehead, he said, "Mrs. Sutherland is here if you need anything. You just give her a shout."

Reaching under the covers, she pulled out a small gold bell. "I can ring this." Giving the bell a quick shake she laughed. "Mrs. Sutherland said that way I won't hurt my throat if I have to yell for her."

Shaking his head at the wonder of his daughter, he left the room listening to the sound of the bell's dinging.

"I'm coming, Laura." Wiping her hands on a dish towel, the woman started to bustle past him.

"You don't need to go she was just showing me how the bell works."

Nodding in understanding, she turned to go back into the kitchen and then seemed to think better of it. "Mr. Judson, might I have a word with you?"

Taking his hat from the hook, Alex paused with his hand on the doorknob.

"I think you should let Miss Lydia visit Laura.

She asks about her all the time and I'm running out of reasons why she can't."

"I know. She asked me this morning if I could bring Lydia over to see her."

"If you don't mind my being so bold; would it be so bad if she stopped by?"

Knowing the housekeeper had his daughter's best interest at heart was the only thing that kept his temper in check. He didn't want Lydia to come here. He didn't like the way his children had become attached to her, and he really didn't like the fact that he found himself missing her as well.

Gruffly he said, "I'll see what I can do."

"Oh and Mr. Judson, you need to take better care of yourself, too. I know you're not eating properly. I leave you all these wonderful casseroles and come back in the morning to find them untouched. And you need to sleep in a bed."

Alex knew she meant well, but her concern did little to brighten his darkening mood. He knew full well how he looked. One glance in the mirror this morning and he'd seen the lines of fatigue etched on his face. The worry creasing his brow, the stubble of beard left on his face from not shaving in two days and barely getting in more than two hours sleep at a stretch.

He was doing his best to keep his family going. Taking care of Laura, helping Robert with his schoolwork at the end of the day, and keeping up with his own work load ate up every minute of his day.

Wondering what else he could possibly do, he offered lamely, "I appreciate your concern." With that he left his housekeeper standing in the doorway frowning and shaking her head at him.

Alexander was going to go to check on the site where the new restaurant was being built. He and Cole had finally managed to hire two workers and they'd been assigned to this job. At least one thing was going in his favor.

He'd walked to the site, right smack in the middle of Main Street, where the building was going up when the sound of feminine laughter caught his attention.

All too late he realized that the laughter belonged to the one woman he'd no desire to speak. She was coming out of Jules' Mercantile with Maggie by her side. Shielded by the corner post of the store, the two of them didn't see him until they were almost in front of him.

Jerking her head up, Lydia looked at him. Ignoring the tug at his heart and the immediate attraction he still felt at the mere sight of her, Alex tipped his hat to her, trying to be all politeness and to keep his true emotions hidden.

"Hello, Alexander."

"Lydia."

"How is Laura feeling?"

A breeze picked up, blowing wispy strands of red hair about her face. Reaching up, Lydia brushed them away.

"Laura is coming along nicely."

He knew his responses were lame and that she was expecting more from him than just one sentence answers, but Alex was still upset.

"I'm glad to hear that. I can send some school work home with Robert if you'd like."

They both knew she wasn't teaching and yet she still had her student's best interest at heart. He felt his resolve melt just a little. Nodding, he said, "That would be fine."

She was looking up at him with questions in her eyes. He knew she was looking for something more from him. Remaining silent, he stared at her and as each moment ticked by, he found it harder and harder not to pull her in his arms.

"Well, if there's nothing else I'd best be going." Taking hold of Maggie's elbow, she would have continued on, except stepping in front of them he blocked their path.

"I need to have a word with you."

With her chin tipped up he caught the uncertainty flaring in her emerald green eyes. "All right."

He saw the flicker of hurt there, too. "Lydia," he began only to have her interrupt him.

"Yes." The word came out on an exhale.

Why hadn't he ever noticed the freckles dancing across her perfect nose before, he wondered as he tried to find a way to ask her to visit Laura. Clearing his throat he began again. "My daughter would like to see you."

At the mention of Laura her features softened. "How is she doing? Tell me the truth, Alexander."

"The doctor tells me she is doing better than expected and hopefully she'll be able to get out of bed next week." Shoving his hands in his pockets, he took a good look at Lydia.

There were dark shadows beneath her eyes as if she too had been suffering through sleepless nights. Knowing what she'd been going through these past few days, he shared her anguish. He longed to tell her this, but couldn't because he didn't deserve her sympathy.

"You can come by today. Mrs. Sutherland will be there in case Laura needs anything."

Catching her bottom lip between her teeth, Lydia seemed to be thinking. "I'd like to stop by later today."

Nodding, he remembered his daughter's request. "Laura asked if you could bring her a peppermint stick. They have become her favorites."

Her features brightened just a bit. "I'll be sure and bring her some."

He started to walk away but turned around. "Lydia?"

Taking a step towards him, she looked as if she were going to touch him, and then thought better of it. "Yes?"

"Don't stay too long. Laura still tires quickly."

She could only stare, dumbfounded, at his retreating back, her heart breaking. She thought she'd seen just a small glimmer of something soft and warm in his brown eyes. But as he walked away from her, she feared what little hope she'd ever had of making him forgive was evaporating like moist dew in the warm morning sun.

Putting her arms around her, Maggie consoled her. "I'm sure he wants to see you again, Lydia. He's still upset that Laura was hurt, that's all."

"It's more than that. I know her falling from the tree must have brought back horrible memories of his wife's death. Those feelings I can understand."

Tears welled up and she fought to keep them at bay. "He's so aloof now, just like when we first met."

"I'm sure as soon as Laura is out of bed he'll come around."

Maggie's words of reassurance did nothing for Lydia. She knew what a stubborn man Alexander could be. Look how long it took him to accept her as schoolteacher, how long it was before he'd opened his home and heart to her.

All of his trust was gone now. She'd seen the skepticism lingering in his eyes.

Squaring her shoulders, Lydia went back in the store to purchase a peppermint stick. Imagining how Robert must be feeling left out in all the attention being given to his sister, she picked up three more. Each of them would have two sticks to keep them happy.

Not bothering to go back to Aunt Margaret's house, Lydia walked over to the Judson's. Mrs. Sutherland was there to meet her at the door.

"Miss Lydia, I know one little girl who's going to be mighty pleased to see you." Holding the door wide, she let Lydia in.

The yellow curtains hanging in the windows fluttered in the breeze. Looking around, Lydia could see the home as always was as neat as a pin. Mrs. Sutherland's love for the family was evident at every turn. It was so hard for her to be here right now, because Lydia had gone so far as to allow herself to imagine how her own loving touches could have transformed this house.

Shaking her head to clear those thoughts from her mind, Lydia thanked Mrs. Sutherland for letting her in. "I saw Alexander today. He gave me permission to stop by."

A frown puckered the older woman's brow. "Oh Miss, I'm sorry he's being so hardheaded."

"Don't apologize for his behavior, Mrs. Sutherland. I deserve it."

Shaking her head furiously, the woman was quick to say, "No you don't. What happened was nothing more than a childhood accident. He of all people should know that. Children do these kinds of things all the time. Why just last year Robert cut himself and needed to be stitched up."

"Yes, but I wasn't here last year. Robert and Laura weren't my responsibility last year." Forlornly, she took the bag of candy from her silk purse.

"At any rate, I brought these peppermint sticks by for them."

"You go ahead on in. She's in her parent's bedroom." Startled that she'd referred to it that way, Mrs. Sutherland quickly amended, "I mean her father's room. Not that the man ever sleeps anymore." She muttered while going back to the kitchen. "I'll fix you a nice cup of tea."

"Thank you." Lydia went down the short hallway stopping in the threshold of the bedroom where Laura lay amidst a pile of pillows and blankets.

Feeling nervous about going into the room that Alex had shared with his wife, Lydia waited for Laura to notice her.

"Hello."

"Miss Lydia, you came!"

Holding the bag of candy out, Lydia said, "And I brought you a little something."

Pushing herself up, Laura sat higher against the hand-carved headboard. "Peppermint sticks I hope."

"Open the bag and see for yourself." Placing the bag in her outstretched hand, Lydia pulled the rocking chair over to the bed and sat.

"Thank you, Miss Lydia."

"Two of them are for your brother."

Wrinkling her little nose, Laura balked, "Do I have to share with him?"

"I'm afraid so, otherwise I'll have to keep them all for myself," Lydia teased.

Tearing the wrapper off one of the striped sticks, Laura happily put it in her mouth. While the little girl enjoyed the treat, Lydia was battling with emotions that threatened to make her run from the house.

"Where have you been?"

Laura's words penetrated the fog in her brain. Frowning Lydia tried to find the right words to answer with.

"I've been helping my family with some projects."

"I missed you."

Her heart was really going to break. "I've missed you too, sweetie." And she truly had missed Laura, and Robert and Alexander. She missed being here in this home; she missed feeling the pitter-patter of her heart every time Alexander Judson was near.

"Why do you look so sad, Miss Lydia?" Tipping her head to one side, Laura was studying her.

"I'm not sad," she lied. Moving to sit beside her on the bed, Lydia reached for one of the books piled next to Laura. "Would you like me to read you a story?"

Nodding, Laura settled back into the pillow.

Turing the page, Lydia began to read from "Goldilocks and the Three Bears" one of Laura's favorites. By the time she'd turned to the last page, the child was sound asleep. Taking the remnants of the peppermint stick from her hand, Lydia placed it on the bag on the nightstand.

Then going into the kitchen she found a clean cloth and after dampening it, went back to wash the stickiness from Laura's hands. While she tended to her, Lydia took the time to admire the long lashes framing her eyelids. Brushing some golden curls off her forehead, Lydia bent to drop a kiss on her smooth brow.

Laura stirred and Lydia pulled the blankets snug around her. When she'd settled into a nice slumber, Lydia left. Thanking Mrs. Sutherland for letting her visit, she was about to leave when she spotted Alex and Robert heading this way.

She couldn't very well avoid them so taking a stand on the front porch, she waited.

Chapter Sixteen

"But, Pa I did my work. Just like the new teacher asked. I swear, Pa." Robert was whining while his father wore a dark expression of disapproval on his face.

"Not according to Mrs. Wendall, you didn't. Now you go on in the house and do the assignment the way she told you to."

His harsh tone took Lydia by surprise. She'd never heard him raise his voice or seen him take a hand to his children. Angry at him because he was taking his frustration out on his children, she folded her arms across her chest, waiting for them to notice her. Robert saw her first.

"Miss Lydia, when are you coming back to school? The new teacher is mean and nobody likes her. Say you'll come back. Please, Miss Lydia? Say you'll do it!"

Taking a seat on the top porch step, she waited for Robert to join her, pointedly ignoring his father. "Look, I can't come back right now. I need to help my family." She hated all this lying and blamed Alexander for it.

How could she expect the children to handle the truth, when she barely understood it herself?

Tucking a finger under his chin, she tipped his head up to look at her, and was struck by the resemblance he bore to his father.

Taking a minute to find her voice, she finally said, "Robert, you listen to me right now. You have to behave for the teacher. You tell your friends that I want them to be good just like you all were for me."

"But, Miss Lydia, we want you to come back!" That he was raising his voice to her shocked her, but what he did next left her in tears.

Throwing his arms about her neck, Robert clung to her like there was no tomorrow. Carefully she touched his wrists, gently pulling his arms from around her.

A choking sound came out and then clearing her throat she managed in a whisper, "Robert, it has to be this way."

Desperately, the boy looked from his father to her and back again. Then gathering himself he ran into the house, slamming the screen door behind him.

Lydia rose from the step and walked by Alexander, unable to look at him. At the edge of his yard she paused. Turning slowly, she faced the only man she'd ever truly loved. From this distance it was hard to read his face. She hoped he was feeling as torn up as she was.

"We are doing this to them, Alexander. You and me, Alexander we're what all this hurting and loneliness is about. How much longer are you willing to let this go on?"

His answer to her was an eerie stony silence.

Watching her walk away from him was getting harder and harder to do. There was no other choice; they would all survive just like they had after Joanna had died.

The rest of his evening passed amidst groans and complaints from both his son and daughter. By the time Mrs. Sutherland left, he was exhausted, cranky and wishing he'd had a bottle of whiskey lying around. A good stiff drink was what he needed right now, something to take the edge off.

Rummaging through the kitchen cupboards he found a corked brown jug. Unplugging it, one good whiff was all it took to tell him that this would do the trick. Taking a glass from behind the sink, he poured the whiskey. After one gulp he dumped the bitter liquor out wondering what his life had come to.

Leaning against the counter, he stared out the kitchen window. Off in the distance the town was settling in for the night. Lanterns began to sputter to life behind the window panes of the homes of customers and what few friends he had.

His life was supposed to have turned out differently. His wife was supposed to be by his side helping him raise their children. They'd talked of adding on to the house and their family. None of those things had been allowed to happen because fate had had something else in store for him.

An image of a certain red-hair green-eyed woman popped into his mind. The way she smiled and the sound of her laughter—the warmth that came from her for nothing more than just her existing.

Try as he may, he couldn't forget Lydia or the feelings she brought out in him. Neither could he forget the way Robert and Laura's faces lit up at the sight of her. Their entire world—no—make that *his* entire world, had been turned upside down from the moment he laid eyes upon her.

Or was it that Alexander's world had been turned right side up instead?

The thought stunned him.

Turning down the wick on the lamp, he walked

out of the kitchen, intending to check on Laura and make sure Robert was asleep. Instead, he found himself standing in the bedroom where Laura was sleeping, holding the picture of Joanna.

He stared at her image for a long time, imploring her to send him some kind of a message to let him know it would be all right to let go. He looked at her for so long and so hard that eventually her image blurred, in it's place he saw a thick mane of brilliant red hair and twinkling green eyes.

Blinking he waited for his imagination to settle down. When Joanna's image returned, he opened the top dresser drawer knowing he had been answer. Pushing aside an aged pink quilt, he made a place for his wife's picture. Gently, he covered the gold frame and closed the drawer.

"Lydia, you simply cannot pack up and leave Surprise! We won't let you."

As fast as she was packing her things in the black trunk, Abigail and Maggie were unpacking them.

"Abigail, I have to do this. Can't you see there's nothing left for me here?" Having a tug of war with Maggie over a dress that she'd already packed three times, Lydia was about ready to flee the house with nothing more than the clothes on her back.

"Frankly, I think you're just being a coward. It's

always been easier for you to run than to stay and fight for what you want," Abigail exclaimed tossing a hand full of undergarments on the already rumpled bed.

Giving up for the moment, Lydia released her hold on the green silk dress sending Maggie flying onto the bed.

Hands on her hips she said, "There. Now I hope you're both happy. Just look at this mess. Aunt Margaret is going to have our hides when she sees this."

None of them had noticed that the bedroom door stood ajar and that Anna and their aunt were just outside in the hallway observing their antics.

"I say now, what's the reason for all of this?" Anna wheeled their aunt into the bedroom. "I want all of this stuff put back in its place and furthermore I'll hear nothing of your leaving Surprise, Lydia!"

Aunt Margaret's normally pale complexion had turned to a fine shade of red.

"I *am* leaving." Stubbornness was her strong suit and Lydia didn't hesitate to use it right now to her full advantage. She had always been the one to hold out the longest and this time it wouldn't be any different.

"No. You are not." Each word was punctuated with a thumping of Aunt Margaret's hand on the arm of her wheelchair.

Maggie and Abigail knew better than to go against her when she was this angry, but Lydia stood her ground refusing to give even an inch.

"Yes, I am. There's nothing left for me to do here. I've resigned from the school and Alexander has made it perfectly clear that there's no place in his life for me." Suddenly tired, she sat on the edge of the bed where her cousins sat flanking her.

Coming over to them, Aunt Margaret said, "Well, he's a fool."

"Then so am I for falling in love with him." Biting her lower lip, Lydia was determined not to cry again. She'd already shed enough tears for Alexander Judson.

The only sound in the room was the ticking of the clock on the fireplace mantle. For a long time none of the women spoke, each mulling over the predicament.

It was Maggie who broke the silence saying, "I for one am glad that I haven't come under the spell of some man. There's more to life than being in love you know."

Staring at her niece like she'd grown an extra head, Aunt Margaret commented dryly, "Your time hasn't come yet, but mark my words, it will."

Before an argument ensued with her namesake, she went on. "Be that as it may, this isn't about you, Maggie, it's about Lydia. We need to figure out how to fix this mess."

Standing, Lydia began to usher them out of her room. "Go, all of you. Leave me in peace." She simply couldn't take their well-meaning pestering anymore.

Once out in the hallway, Margaret looked at the three women. "Anna go hitch up the buggy. Maggie you stay here—and under no circumstances is Lydia to know that I've left the house. Abigail you come with me."

Twenty minutes later a disheveled housekeeper, one sheriff and a riled-up old woman were on Alexander's doorstep. Knocking on the door, Margaret waited impatiently in the cool evening air for the man to let her in.

When he finally did step out on the porch, Margaret knew why Lydia had fallen for this man. With his tall frame silhouetted against the backdrop of his home, Alexander Judson presented one mighty handsome figure.

Lazily, as if he hadn't a care in the world, Alexander leaned his shoulder up against one of the porch posts. "Forgive me if I don't ask you ladies in, but my children have finally settled in for the night and I don't want them disturbed."

Leaning heavily on her cane, Margaret squinted at him. "You could at least let me sit in that rocking chair." With a quick twitch of her hand she indicated the slate back rocker on the porch.

Stepping aside he acquiesced, helping her up the

steps. Though she really didn't require his assistance, it never hurt to put on a good show. Once settled, she huffed, "I think you're being way too hard on Lydia."

"You sure don't beat around the bush, do you, Miss Margaret?"

"There's no time for chitchat. Lydia didn't mean for your daughter to get hurt. And I know you're pushing her away because you can't abide by your own guilty conscious."

Off in the distance a coyote howled. Its plaintive cry echoed down the valley. Alexander slowly turned to look at her.

"I know it was an accident, and you know why the entire incident upset me."

"Yes, I do. You were late meeting Joanna, just as you were for your picnic with Lydia and the children. Tell me something, Alexander. Do you want to spend the rest of your life alone?"

"I don't see how that's any of your business."

"Where my nieces are concerned, I make it my business. You know I'd have thought by now that your friend Cole Stanton would have told you as much."

"I know all about how he and the sheriff hooked up." He was of course referring to the not-so-subtle interference of Margaret Monroe Sinclair on behalf of Sheriff Abigail.

Raising an eyebrow, he looked at her. "I don't think Lydia and I need to be locked up together."

"Oh that. Well, it was what Cole and Abigail needed. They ended up living happily ever after. Don't you want that?"

"Happily ever after?" Snorting, he shook his head. "I don't think it's in the cards for me."

"Alexander, if you really want to raise your children alone, to live here in this cozy home all by yourself with no one to warm your bed, no one to share your day with—to share your life with, well then so be it. But if you don't want that, then for goodness sakes forgive yourself. Tell Lydia what happened on the day Joanna died. Let her back into your life."

When silence greeted her, she added, "She's a wonderful woman and you could do worse." The rocker creaked as she rose and walked down the steps.

Pausing near the buggy she added, "You should know that she's planning on leaving Surprise in the morning."

Chapter Seventeen

Lydia was leaving? Alexander didn't know what to think. Stuffing his hands in his pockets, he returned to the house, closing the door behind him. He stood there wondering, did he really want her to leave, to never see her again?

Sitting in the chair where he'd spent more lonely nights than he cared to remember, Alex stared at a cold fireplace wondering what his life had become. The more he stared at the empty space where a warm fire should be lit, the more he realized what his life was fast turning into.

Soon it would be no different than the cold empty hearth and he realized with a start that he wanted warmth in his life. He *needed* the warmth that only one woman could bring. Enough wallowing in self-pity, shame, guilt—he knew what had to be done.

Wishing with all his heart it hadn't taken him so long to come to terms with Joanna's death and Laura's accident, Alex finally allowed himself forgiveness. A strange, newfound peace settled around him, making him feel something he hadn't felt in a very long time. Hope.

It seemed like ages before Mrs. Sutherland appeared on his doorstep. Not waiting for her to enter, he ran past her, the sun warm and bright on his face.

"Mr. Judson, where are you off to in such a hurry?" she called after him.

"You'll find out soon enough!" he shouted over his shoulder. His feet couldn't carry him fast enough. Lengthening his stride, he sprinted up the hill to Miss Margaret's big stone house.

Pounding on the massive door, he was glad Anna didn't waste any time letting him in. "Where's Lydia? I need to speak with her."

"She's upstairs in her room."

Taking the steps two at a time, he reached the upper floor just as Lydia was coming out of a room to his right. The sight of her took his breath away. Alex felt his heart swell. Walking to her, he reached out, laying his hand on her cheek.

"What brings you by, Alexander?" she asked, her voice barely audible.

Pulling Lydia closer to him, he lowered his head so their foreheads were touching. "I heard you were leaving."

"And you came to say good-bye." Her lips moved against his cheek.

Shaking his head, he wrapped his arms around her, pulling her close against his chest. "I came to see if there was anything I could do to make you stay."

Pulling back just a little, she looked up into those dark eyes. Lightly tracing the deep lines along his cheekbones she said, "Tell me you love me."

Cupping her chin with one hand he met her gaze. "I love you, Lydia Louise Monroe."

"Oh, Alex I love you too, more than anyone I've ever known."

Holding her tighter, he said, "I'm sorry for acting like such an idiot these past weeks."

Smiling up at him, she said, "You should be sorry. I feared my heart would be broken forever."

Taking him by the hand, she led him into her bedroom. Laughing when he saw the mess, Alex said, "You were really leaving."

"I was."

"Why?"

The corners of her mouth drooped. "I couldn't stay without you." Toying with one of the many petticoats heaped on the bed, she continued, "I can't compete with a ghost, Alexander. And I can't bear it when you keep your deepest feelings buried."

Swallowing hard, he thought about what she was saying. For so long he'd kept his emotions locked up. This was the most difficult thing he'd done since burying Joanna.

He knew then and there the time had come to move on, to let love into his life once more.

"Lydia, you are the ray of sunshine that has been missing from my life—from Robert's and Laura's lives for too long."

She stopped fingering the white cotton cloth to stare at him. Her green eyes widened in surprise.

"I've never met anyone as passionate as you are about life. Lydia, your passion just overflows. It's there in everything you do, from the way you dress, to the way you teach, to the way you love."

When she still didn't say anything, he kept going. "You came into this town like a tornado; a whirl of silk and fiery red hair ready to take on the world. You scared me, Lydia."

Her eyebrows rose at the statement. "And I was nothing like Joanna?"

He shook his head. "You are so different. It's hard to explain. Joanna, she lived life, and you love life."

"Alexander, tell me about the day she died."

Pain cut through him like the steel edge of a knife. He had faced this alone for so long and he wasn't sure how to begin to talk about the feelings that had been running around inside of him.

Her voice reached out to him, imploring him to bare his soul. "We need to get this out in the open. You need to talk about her death so we can be together."

"The pond was her favorite place, it's the reason we built the house there. I was supposed to meet her there, but the wheel on my wagon broke a few miles out of town, and I was late."

Scrubbing his hand over his face, he looked at Lydia, "I was late. And she was just lying there with blood all over her face. Laura was crying, Robert was still asleep. Thankfully, he never saw a thing."

"And you blamed yourself for her death. All this time and you couldn't see it was just an accident?"

"My life was finally falling into order and then Laura fell. I was late for your picnic and she fell from the tree. I never blamed you. I blamed myself for being late, for letting my work take over my life."

"And you saw it as your wife's death all over again." Rushing to him, Lydia threw her arms about his neck. "Oh, Alexander I am so, so very sorry."

"I should have told you how guilty I felt. I couldn't bear my shame. This was never about my not trusting you. I took the coward's way out, pushing you away because I thought it would be easier to not see you than to face what I had done and for that I need your forgiveness."

Hugging him close, she said, "I'm so sorry for everything and there is nothing for me to forgive."

Smoothing her hair back, he cupped her face in his hands. "Marry me, Lydia."

"Oh, Alexander." Raining kisses all over his face, Lydia said yes. "Yes, yes, yes!" she shouted for the whole world to hear.

"What do you think Robert and Laura are going to say when we tell them our news?" Lydia wanted everything to be perfect.

Grinning at her, Alexander replied, "Let's go find out." They had to run the gauntlet of her family first, and after accepting hasty congratulations, managed to be out of the house within a few minutes.

Hand in hand, they walked up the hill to Alexander's home. Robert was sitting on the porch forlornly tossing handfuls of pebbles into the flower garden and Laura was in the rocker, her arm propped up on a pillow. From the kitchen came the sounds of dishes scrapping together, Mrs. Sutherland was preparing the noonday meal.

"Hey, Pa." Tossing another handful of pebbles on the ground, Robert barely looked up.

"Miss Lydia!" Squealing in delight, Laura dropped the pillow to the porch floor and scrambled off the chair. "Miss Lydia, I've missed you so much."

Lydia barely caught Laura as she flung herself off the top porch step and into her waiting arms. "I've missed you too, pumpkin."

"Can you stay long?"

"As long as you'd like. Your father and I have something to tell you."

Grumbling, Robert asked, "Is it good or bad?"

Sitting beside his son, Alexander brushed the dust off of Robert's pant legs. "I think you're going to like our news."

Lydia sat on the bottom step pulling the young girl onto her lap. Leaning back against the railing, she smiled at Robert. "Your father has asked me to marry him and I said yes."

"You mean it?"

Nodding, she grinned. "Cross my heart."

Squirming around to face them, Laura laughed. "We're going to be a family."

Robert was hugging his father and Mrs. Sutherland stepped out onto the porch wiping her hands on the front of the apron she wore. "Did I hear right? We're going to have a wedding?"

"Yes, ma'am." Alex stood to accept her congratulations.

"I daresay it's about time you came to your senses."

Their wedding took place two weeks later with the entire town serving as witness to their vows. Lydia had never felt so happy. The party that followed went on long into the night. With Robert and Laura off to spend a few nights with Aunt Margaret, the newlyweds were left by themselves at the house.

Wedding gifts were piled high on the kitchen table. Having already rifled through most of them, Lydia laughed when she opened Mrs. Drumm's gift.

"Oh my, what a nice surprise. And here I thought the woman disliked me." Pushing the tissue paper aside, she showed her husband a silver letter opener engraved with the letter "J".

"I meant to ask you about that. Why don't the two of you get along?"

"She thinks I spent too much time admiring a certain mill owner and not enough time with the students. I think it was that whole 'I'm too passionate about life' thing."

Kissing her, he smiled. "I'm glad you're passionate."

Rising, she took his hand. Lydia pulled them to a stop in front of the fireplace where a small fire was burning, admiring the wood carving Cole had made for their wedding gift.

The statue stood about five inches high and was of a hummingbird, its long beak burrowing into the petal of a flower. Lydia couldn't help admiring the intricate carving. The bird reminded her of how her life had been before Alexander when she'd been busy flitting from one thing to the next, never staying put in any one place for very long.

Alex wrapped her in his arms. Bending his head, he nuzzled her neck. "Umm, that feels good," she murmured.

Softly, with her gaze still on the hummingbird, Lydia began to talk. "When I came here to Surprise it was for adventure and fun. I never imagined myself a schoolteacher. I guess I thought I would while away my days taking tea with Aunt Margaret, visiting with Abigail and Maggie."

Alex pulled her closer.

"I wasn't thinking about falling in love. This isn't where I thought I'd be." Turning in his arms to face him, she whispered against the warmth of his lips, "But I'm glad to be here."

"That makes two of us."

Taking her hand in his, Lydia followed her husband down the short hallway to their bedroom where they would begin their new life and she would share all of her passion with him.

23706334R00104

Made in the USA
Charleston, SC
30 October 2013